Pride and Prejudice at the Cat Café

Pride and Prejudice at the Cat Café

a Furrever Friends Sweet Romance

by Kris Bock

Sign up for Kris Bock's newsletter to get a free 30-page story set in the world of the Furrever Friends cat café. You'll also get a printable copy of "22 recipes from the cat café" and a short story from the Accidental Detective humorous mystery series. Sign up at sendfox.com/KrisBock

This book includes four recipes and two preview chapters at the end.

Pig River Press

Chapter 1

"It is a truth universally acknowledged that a man in possession of a fortune can be convinced to donate to a special needs cat rescue."

Liz paused in brushing the cream and white cat in her lap and glanced over at her friend Jade. "What?"

"Rich guy. Money for cat rescue." Jade jumped up and started pacing. The cat café wasn't the easiest place to pace, since the twenty-by-forty-foot space had half a dozen small tables with chairs in addition to the long benches under the windows, several tall cat towers, and a giant version of a hamster wheel. Not to mention several patrons eating, drinking, or playing with cats, in addition to the cats napping in hammocks or on the benches, and the sleek Bengal racing in the wheel.

"Ah, your potential donor. Well, I hope he's rich enough to fund care for every needy kitten in town." Liz pulled a clump of cat hair from the brush and added it to the growing pile beside her. "Like the extra one I'm making here. I'm surprised there's any fur left on the cat."

"That toasted marshmallow is Lydia," Jade said. "Her supply of floof is endless. And actually, the guy I'm meeting isn't rich himself, as far as I know. But he works for the Anderson family charitable foundation, and I know they're cat lovers. They started Big Cat Rescue."

Liz had been meaning to visit that place since it opened but hadn't managed it yet. She told herself she didn't have time. Some days she even believed that was the main reason.

"That has wild animals, or animals that should be wild," Liz said. "Lions and things, not house cats."

Jade stopped pacing long enough to smooth her hand down the back of a black cat snoozing on a platform. "Have you ever seen a lion with a big cardboard box? Cats are cats."

"I guess." Liz stroked the brush over the purring cat. It was oddly relaxing. She hadn't understood why people would pay to go to a cat café and hang out with cats. She was starting to get it. She didn't want the extra responsibility of pets until her life was more settled. Jade often fostered rescues, but for someone who didn't have a roommate like her, this was a nice alternative. Maybe Liz wasn't the only one who needed the stress relief of hanging out with animals but couldn't commit to one of their own at the moment. Plus the café was known for its excellent bakery and menu of hot drinks.

"Thanks for inviting me here," Liz added. "I needed a break. And now I feel like I'm actually accomplishing something today, even if the only result is a better-groomed cat."

"Some days that's the best you can hope for." Jade grabbed her mug and downed the last of her latte before resuming her pacing.

Liz had rarely seen her friend anything but placid and cheerful. Either the caffeine in the latte was hitting her hard, or she was nervous about this meeting. Liz tried to think of something supportive to say but came up blank. She was too tired and frustrated to be optimistic, even on Jade's behalf.

Jade put one knee on the bench that ran along the wall and peered out the window. Apparently she didn't see the guy she was supposed to be meeting outside, because she turned back and plopped down next to Liz with a sigh.

"Distract me," Jade said. "I know you're not supposed to ask a grad student when their dissertation will be done."

"Unless you want to make them cry."

"So I'll only invite you to vent if you need to, and if you don't want to talk about it during the few hours a week you take off, that's fine too."

"I don't."

"Totally understandable." Jade gestured at the cat in

Liz's lap. "So, Lydia is one of five siblings the café got from the shelter this week."

Words burst out of Liz. "Dr. Bennett is driving me around the bend! I've spent a year working on this study, and now she wants me to go in a completely new direction. You don't need to smirk at me. I know I just said I didn't want to talk about it."

"But maybe you need to?"

"I guess." Liz slumped back. "I want to forget about it for a couple of hours. But I can't believe she's doing this again."

"What's her reasoning for asking you to change focus?"

"The direction we were going isn't working. The evidence doesn't support our theory."

"*Our* theory? You mean *her* theory?"

"Well, the theory that was supposed to be the basis for my dissertation."

"Didn't you already change that theory at her suggestion?"

"Twice."

"And isn't the point of science to test a theory and find out the answer, right or wrong? Not necessarily to come up with evidence that supports a particular theory?"

"You should have gone into law," Liz grumbled. "Yes, I argued that I could get a solid dissertation from the research we've already done. But ..."

"But she doesn't want you to get your PhD. She wants you to keep working on her research."

Liz whimpered and rubbed her face. "Yes. But I don't know what to do about it."

"What about your other advisors?"

"Oh, they're okay. Benjie says he'll sign off on everything as soon as Dr. Bennett does. I think he's tired of her too. He claims he would've approved the last two versions, although I guess it's easy for him to say that and let Dr. Bennett take the heat. And Doctor Gardiner is on sabbatical right now. I was supposed to finish before she left, but at this rate she'll be back before I'm ready to defend, so it doesn't make sense to get someone else. Dr. Bennett is the only problem."

"Would those two support you if you insisted on writing the dissertation based on what you have now?"

"I don't know. It feels like whining or tattling to Dad when Mom already said no. Never mind. Tell me about the new kittens." Two of them were wrestling on the floor. Another was crawling along the back of the bench stalking Jade's ponytail.

"They're three months old. We have Jane, Elizabeth, Mary, Catherine, and the one you're brushing is Lydia."

"Catherine I get—Cat for short—but the other names are kind of old-fashioned and human, aren't they?"

Jade scooped up the kitten on the back of the bench and tucked it under her chin as she looked at Liz. "It is a truth universally acknowledged that kittens as cute as these will find a new home quickly."

"They are cute. You said something like that earlier, the universal truth bit."

"It is a truth universally acknowledged?"

"Yeah, that. It's from something, right?"

"Only *Pride and Prejudice*!"

"Right. I think I saw the movie awhile back."

Jade put the back of her free hand to her forehead like a melodramatic silent movie heroine. "Heathen! Philistine!"

"Look, I know it's a book." She was pretty sure it was by Jane Austen and not one of the Brontë sisters but not sure enough to say it out loud and risk more ridicule. "I just haven't read it."

"Well, you ought to. The cat café is going to show one of the movie adaptations for their weekly Mewvie Nights. They figured giving the new kittens Jane Austen character names would be fun and might help them get adopted sooner. They're named after the Bennett daughters in *Pride and Prejudice*."

Jane Austen then. Good. The kitten Jade had identified as Lydia flopped on her back and attacked the brush.

"She's feisty," Liz said, tickling the kitten. "I can't wait till I'm done with this degree and have time for pets of my own. You made the right decision getting out when you did." Not that Liz envied her best friend and roommate or anything.

"You know, it's not too late for you," Jade said. "You're allowed to quit any time."

"I can't give up! I've come so far. I'm so close."

"Are you? It doesn't sound like it, as long as Dr. Bennett can make you do her work."

"She can't keep me here forever." Liz wasn't entirely sure of that. Dr. Bennett had a reputation for ten-year PhD students. "Anyway my parents would be disappointed if I left. I don't want to be a quitter."

"I haven't heard you say anything about *you* wanting to keep going." Jade hesitated. "You do still want to study animal behavior, right?"

"Of course." Liz could hardly stop now, after all the time she'd put in.

"There's no 'of course' about it. People change. Lots of people don't go into the field they originally studied." Jade gestured at herself. "Witness me. And I know having parents with PhDs puts pressure on you to get one too."

Liz didn't want to talk about parental pressure. Anyway, she did still love her field of study. Mostly. When she wasn't angry and frustrated and burned out.

She focused on the simplest complaint. "I just want to be done with school and this stupid, never-ending dissertation! I want to get an actual reasonable salary for going out in the field to study animal behavior. I want to be the principal researcher rather than someone else's gopher and bottle washer."

"Okay," Jade said gently. "Then you'll get there."

"I got through my bachelor's degree in four years. It

wasn't easy, but I did it. Even the master's was a piece of cake. Okay, granted, it was like a seven-layer wedding cake covered in fondant flowers—making one, not eating one—but I managed it. I'm going to stop with the cake analogy before it gets out of hand."

"Good plan. And now I want cake."

As if on cue, a young man pushed through the door from the café area into the cat lounge. "You ladies need anything else?"

"Not until after my meeting," Jade said. "Then I'm going to want a piece of the highest calorie dessert you have. Can you set something aside for us?"

He gave a theatrical bow. "As you wish."

Liz watched him leave. He was cute, in a friendly, golden retriever kind of way.

"Dustin has a girlfriend," Jade said. "One of the other baristas."

"I can still look. Anyway, he's too young for me."

Jade scoffed. "Yeah, because you're ancient."

"I feel it. If I don't get this stupid dissertation finished soon ..." Liz didn't know how to end that sentence. She thought she'd be doing field research before she hit thirty. Thirty was an arbitrary age, simply a round number. But it had passed, with no time or money for a party and disappointed noises from her parents because she wasn't on the faculty of a prestigious university yet, like they were, never mind that they hadn't gotten tenured positions until closer to forty. Now Liz had the sickening sensation that she might be stuck with Dr. Bennett until she was forty.

Something caught Jade's attention through the windows. "That's him." She bolted upright and tried to brush the cat hair off her sweater.

"I didn't realize this was a hot date," Liz teased.

"Of the professional variety. We're going over the proposal I sent him for funding a special needs wing of the rescue. I figured the café is more comfortable but still thematic. Plus he sees one way our cats find their forever homes."

Liz already knew that but didn't complain. She'd too often forgotten or missed what Jade was doing because she was caught up in her own work or exhausted from it.

"Don't worry about the cat hair then. It makes you look authentic." Liz stood and gave her friend's shoulders a quick squeeze. "You got this."

The cat room was separated from the food-service part of the café by a wall with windows. Once people got their food, they could come into the cat room, or if they were fussy about getting cat hair in their food and drink, they could sit at the counter that ran under the windows and look in at the cats.

A group entered the café area from outside: two men, probably in their mid-thirties, and a younger woman. One of the men looked through the windows and waved at Jade. The group paused at the café counter and spoke to the barista there before coming into the cat room.

Both men wore suits, but the resemblance ended there. One was blond and smiling, while the other had dark hair and an expression that said he expected to be disappointed and so he always was.

As they got closer, Liz adjusted her first guess at ages. The men looked closer to Jade and Liz's age, maybe a year or two older. She tended to forget that some people looked adult at thirty, especially when they were wearing suits and had haircuts that probably cost a hundred dollars. She was still a broke student, so she trimmed her hair herself and was currently wearing yoga leggings and an oversized t-shirt. Her day off clothes were only slightly more casual than what she wore to the lab.

The woman with them was younger, maybe twenty. She looked like a student, if you were talking about the students who had money and spent time on their appearance. Liz didn't pay much attention to popular brands, let alone expensive ones, but either the young woman had a lot of money, or she made the things she wore look fashionable and expensive regardless.

Liz suddenly felt dowdy. She pushed aside the feeling. She didn't need to impress anyone, fortunately. She was merely here to relax with some cats.

Jade flashed her high-wattage smile and shook hands with the blonde guy. "Mr. Bingham? I'm Jade."

"Please, call me Carl." He shook her hand with an equally warm smile. "I hope you don't mind, but I brought my sister and our friend. When Caroline heard about the cat café, she couldn't wait to see it."

The young woman tucked her hand through the other guy's arm. "Look, Willie, isn't this just the sweetest place!"

He glanced down at Caroline. "I wish you wouldn't call me that." He looked toward Jade and Liz but didn't offer his hand, perhaps because his right arm was currently locked in the girl's grip. "It's William, please, or Will, if you must."

"Hi William! I'm Jade, and this is my roommate."

Liz broke in. "You can ignore me. I'm just here for the cats."

Caroline took her at her word, not even glancing at her. "Let's leave Carl to his meeting and play with some kittens," she told William.

"I wasn't prepared for this." William studied the room with a look of distaste, as if they'd scheduled the meeting in a porta-potty instead of a perfectly nice café. Even the litter boxes were in a separate room, accessible to the cats through pet flaps. "You play with the cats," he told Caroline. "I'll wait for our orders."

He tried to move away from Caroline, but she came with him like an octopus that wasn't about to give up its prey.

"You don't need to do that. They'll bring stuff in here." Caroline pouted in a coquettish way.

A spot in Liz's temple throbbed. She'd been a teaching assistant for a couple of years. Each semester seemed to have at least one or two smart, hard-working students who chased Liz down after every assignment and test, trying to argue their way from an A-minus to an A-plus. The guys tended to argue that they knew the right answer, so they should get points for it even if they hadn't put it on paper. Meanwhile, that big-eyed pout was a key part of the technique for certain female students. Liz never could convince them that a 4.0 GPA might have helped them get into college, but their grades wouldn't matter much in the real world. the important thing was to learn the material.

Well, Liz didn't have to deal with Caroline, fortunately. The girl might be cooing about the cats, but the way she hung on William suggested she was staking her claim. Did she really think she needed to protect her boyfriend—or imaginary boyfriend—from the people her brother met for a business meeting at a cat café?

The cat Lydia started winding around William's ankles. He grimaced, looking as if a stranger was trying to use his shirt as a handkerchief.

"See, she likes you!" Caroline squealed.

"I swear that cat is boy crazy," Jade said. "She'll take attention from anyone, but if there's a man around, she'll ignore every woman in the room."

"I'm really more of a dog person," William muttered.

Well, that explained it. Liz liked dogs too. And cats and rabbits and ferrets and rats. Also monkeys, lemurs, red pandas, tree kangaroos, otters, elephants, dolphins, and just about every other animal.

Except for people. She didn't always have a high opinion of them.

Liz scooped up Lydia. "I'll distract her for a while. It looks like your drinks are here." She jerked her chin toward the door as Dustin came in with a tray.

Lydia squirmed and meowed, wanting to get back to pestering the handsome man. Liz strode to the far side of the room and deposited Lydia on top of a cat tree. "Behave yourself," Liz muttered. "You don't want a guy like that anyway. A dogs-only person!”

Lydia sat up and began grooming, ostentatiously ignoring Liz.

Liz huffed out a breath. “Don’t bother making yourself pretty for some man. If he doesn’t adore you at your worst, he’s not worth it.” She avoided looking toward that group again.

Chapter 2

William drank herbal tea, because he never had caffeine after 2:00 p.m. How had he gotten himself into this? If he'd realized they were going to a cat café, he would have taken his allergy medicine first. Or he wouldn't have gone at all, if he'd known Caroline was coming too.

When William and Carl were teens, and little Caroline followed them around, it was cute. Now she was twenty and seemed determined to get William to see her in a new, romantic light. He cringed at the thought. Not only would it be weird to date his best friend's much younger sister, whom he'd known almost since she was born, but she was immature and spoiled and prone to high pitched giggling and shrieking that made William want to renounce all worldly pleasures and become a hermit.

But Carl wanted to keep an eye on his sister, who'd gotten too into partying at college and was now on probation, and little Caroline still wanted to hang out with the older boys. William couldn't bring himself to tell Carl that he'd rather avoid Caroline. No doubt it would get better over time, as she matured and got tired of throwing herself against William's disinterest.

At the moment, she was squealing with girlish delight, too loud to be entirely natural. She pounced on one cat and then another, petting them or trying to get them to play, but she kept shooting flirtatious looks at William, wanting him to join in.

He wanted to walk out instead, but Carl was deep in conversation with the pretty blond woman, Jade. William didn't want to interrupt and couldn't just leave without some kind of explanation or excuse.

But he had to get some distance from Caroline. She was leaning over a chair, her rear pointing toward William and wiggling, as she made baby talk to a calico cat that radiated indifference.

William stepped up beside her. "You should sit down and see if that cat will climb into your lap. You could get a good photo for your ..."

He couldn't remember which social media platform she spent so much time on. She'd told him, repeatedly asking him to follow her, which was one more reason he had avoided whatever it was.

"Your stream," he finished, hoping that was clear enough without suggesting more interest than he really felt.

"Oh, what a great idea! William, you're so clever. Here, take my phone." She got settled with the cat and he framed the image. "We should do a whole series here," she said. "Maybe some videos of me and the cats, or the two of us—"

He handed the phone back. "That's not my kind of thing, but have fun."

Before she could respond, he turned and—well, not *scurried*, exactly, but he strode quickly across the room. If he was very lucky, Caroline would not want to disturb the cat on her lap, or she'd take his hint gracefully—or more likely, she'd be lured in by the idea of getting social media content. But William didn't dare stand around doing nothing, or he risked getting drawn back in, so headed toward the woman who had taken that fluffy little cat to the far side of the room.

He stopped beside her. "Hi." He blinked a couple of times. He'd been so focused on dodging Caroline that he hadn't planned what he would say to this person. He wasn't good with spontaneous small talk. He managed to come up with, "So do you work here?"

She gave him a cool look. "No. I'm taking a break from my PhD dissertation work."

"Oh? That's nice." He shoved his hands in his pockets and reminded himself not to hunch his shoulders.

Had he insulted her by asking if she worked at a cat café? It was probably a nice place to work, assuming you tolerated cats better than he could. But he'd met some PhDs who were pretty snobbish about their degrees. And he worked with one guy who'd balked at learning new calendar software, as if he'd filled up his brain and had no more room, or he'd put in his time and shouldn't be asked to study anything again, ever.

It would probably be natural to ask this woman about her degree program or area of study next. But then he risked hearing a long lecture by someone who didn't realize she was using industry-specific lingo that meant nothing to the average person. No matter how much he wanted to avoid Caroline, that sounded like a frying pan/fire dilemma.

He couldn't think of anything else to say. The fluffy cat scrambled down from its perch to wind around his ankles again. The woman gave it a disappointed look, as if the cat should know better than to fraternize with William. But of course he was the cat's favorite person. They knew when someone was allergic. He was only surprised he didn't have every cat in the room crawling all over him.

A large orange cat sat in one of the cat trees close to eye level. William looked in that general direction, but really he was studying the woman from the corner of his vision. She was pretty too, in a very different way from her friend. She had dark hair and eyes, her features sharper and her expression more cynical. He had a weakness for snarky, cynical women. He didn't know what that said about him and preferred not to ask.

Then he realized the orange cat, which he'd been pretending to watch, was licking its genitals. His face heated and he shifted his gaze to some paintings—of cats, of course—on the side wall.

She must have decided the silence was too awkward. She said, "So you're friends with Mr. Bingham."

"He'd want you to call him Carl. Mr. Bingham is his father." He tried to chuckle but it came out a kind of hoarse wheeze. That must be because of the cat dander. Definitely not because he was nervous and his voice was breaking like a teenage boy. Oh, well. The comment wasn't that funny anyway.

"Do you work with him?" she asked.

He opened his mouth to answer, but a tickle built up in his nose. He stared at her for a few seconds, trying desperately to convince himself he didn't need to sneeze.

She frowned. "Because I don't work with the shelter or the café, so maybe you should be over in the business meeting, instead of ... whatever it is you're trying to do here."

He pulled out a handkerchief, turned away, and rubbed vigorously at his nose. When he was relatively sure he wouldn't sneeze in her face, he turned back.

"No, I avoid the charity stuff." William cleared his throat, which was starting to itch. Where was his tea? Oh, he'd put it down to take Caroline's picture, and he wasn't going back over there now. "Carl and I are old friends, and we usually go out for dinner on Friday nights. I didn't realize he planned to come here first."

And William might have a few words for Carl about that. Why hadn't he warned William about the cats? Maybe he didn't realize William's allergies would act up so badly in such a short time. It had been ages since William had been caught around cats unprepared. He'd almost forgotten how bad it could get.

William shook away the thought. "Anyway. I'm William."

"Yes, I heard." She took a step away and started petting a gray cat sprawled on a table.

She'd missed his hint, so he clarified. "But I didn't get your name."

Her eyes widened while the rest of her face went still, as if he'd caught her in a lie or something instead of just pointing out that her name hadn't come up in their introductions, probably because Caroline had distracted everyone.

The woman's mouth pressed into a thin line for a second before she said, "I'm Liz. But you don't have to ..." She waved her hand in a vague way that gave him no idea of what he didn't have to do. "If you don't need to be in that meeting, you can ... I guess you don't like cats, but the coffee is good."

"Tea," he said. "Well, probably the coffee is good as well. I don't know. I'm sure everything's fine. And as far as the cats go—"

He wanted to explain that he *liked* cats, but because of his allergies, he liked them at a distance.

Something landed on his shoulder. He jerked in surprise and swung around, expecting to see a cat responding to the challenge by getting as close to William's face as possible.

But no, it was much worse.

Caroline looked up at him through her lashes. She was talking again, but he didn't catch the words, since his attention was still on Liz as she grumbled, "I knew you'd find something more entertaining here." She moved away.

As Caroline prattled—how could she not see that behavior that had been cute when she was six was not so endearing when she was twenty?—William reflected on his conversation with Liz. He hadn't shown himself to his best advantage. In fact, it was probably a long way from his top 100 first impressions. Not that he needed to impress her. She wasn't anyone important—important to his world, at least; no doubt she was important in her own world, whatever that was. Not the cat café or cat rescue, apparently.

But as far as William was concerned, Liz was merely someone he'd met briefly in a place he'd never expected to be. He was only there because Carl and Jade had apparently decided this was an appropriate place for a business meeting.

William spent a moment watching them. She didn't look like a Jade. She should have an old-fashioned name, Eleanor or Florence, to go with the porcelain shepherdess coloring and soft curves. She also didn't look like she was petitioning for money, what with the cream-colored sweater over dark pants, but if she worked at a cat rescue, she probably didn't have much need for business suits.

Come to think of it, Carl didn't look like he was in a business meeting either, despite his suit. The two of them leaned toward each other with big smiles, the paperwork seemingly forgotten on the table between them. From a distance, that looked much more like a date going very well than a serious business meeting.

But then Carl always had that sunny, outgoing disposition that turned everyone into a friend. It meant people sometimes tried to take advantage of him. Then William would have to step in, play the bad guy, and get things sorted out so Carl wouldn't be hurt. Sometimes he envied Carl his cheerful amiability. Once in a while William even wished *he* had someone to play the bad guy on his behalf. But not everyone could be like Carl, so William would play his role as needed and be grateful that Carl's generosity extended to friendship with a socially awkward guy he'd known since childhood.

William would even put up with Caroline. He wasn't tolerant by nature, but he only had a few close friends, so he tried to do whatever they needed of him.

He came back from his thoughts to realize Caroline had wound herself around his arm again and was silently looking up at him. She'd pushed her lips into the full pout he was probably supposed to find cute, but her narrowed gaze suggested annoyance. He had no idea what she'd been saying.

She broke the silence. "You're not listening to me."

"I'm sorry." He'd apologize, because he'd been rude, but he didn't want to encourage her to repeat herself. "My allergies are really acting up. I'm going to wait outside. Or maybe I'll take a walk and see you two at the restaurant later."

Caroline rubbed her lips together. "I wanted you to take more pictures of me."

"Can't do that!" He was glad his voice came out in a croak to prove his point. "I need fresh air."

"I guess I can walk with you."

"No, no, you don't want to pass up this opportunity." William looked around wildly. Only a few other people were in the room at the moment: two older women sitting at a table sharing a piece of pie, a man at another table typing away at a laptop, and a boy of about thirteen who seemed to be more of a draw for the cats than William usually was. The boy had half a dozen cats sitting on him, rubbing up against him, or otherwise within reach.

What William really wanted was a good-looking male college student who'd be delighted to spend time with Caroline, but he chose the boy as the best option.

"Let's see if he can help." William twisted out of Caroline's grasp, crossed the short distance to the boy, and smiled. "You look like you know a lot of the cats here."

The boy nodded. "All of them. I'm here every day."

William's eyes widened at that. This didn't seem like a typical teen hang out.

"My mom is the baker," the boy explained. "I'm Brian."

"Excellent. My friend could use your help." William gestured at Caroline, who looked vaguely annoyed. "She wants some pictures of herself with the cats. I'll bet you know how to use the phone camera better than I do, and—" He broke off to cough. "I really need to get out of here. Bye!"

He fled Caroline and the allergens without glancing back. He was halfway down the block before he realized he'd walked away from Liz in the middle of the conversation. Oh well, she was probably glad to be rid of him.

Chapter 3

On Sunday morning, Liz closed her computer and rubbed her throbbing forehead. Jade had been singing for the last hour. It was like living with freaking Cinderella, the Disney version where she had all the animal friends and was unfailingly cheerful when she should have been enraged by her mistreatment.

But Liz would not go into a rant in her own mind. What was the point of arguing with someone who agreed with you?

Anyway, apparently Jade had a reason for singing. Carl had liked her business proposal. Carl understood that while the local cat rescue was on sound footing, it didn't have the resources to handle special needs cats. Carl loved cats. Carl, Carl, Carl.

Liz had to smile, seeing her friend so giddy. She just hoped Carl was the sincere and not merely showing enthusiasm because he wanted to impress Jade long enough to get her into bed. If he was playing games, Liz would have to destroy him, and she didn't have time for that. But he'd seemed nice enough.

Once she'd shaken off her annoyance at the cat-hater and the squealing girl desperately trying to attract him, Liz had watched Jade and Carl with great interest. The chemistry between them had been off the charts. Liz might have envied Jade for that too.

Not that she envied her best friend for anything. She wanted wonderful things for Jade, and Liz didn't have time for a relationship anyway, or know anyone interesting, so ...

Wait, what had she been thinking about?

Jade hit a particularly high note.

Oh, right. Good chemistry.

Liz chuckled and headed to the kitchen to refill her coffee. She was pretty sure she'd already taken the last cup, but if she was lucky, Jade would have started a second pot. She found Jade scrubbing the counters as she sang. Liz scowled at the coffee maker, or more specifically the empty space where the glass pot should be. The dishwasher was running; apparently Jade had decided to wash the coffee pot as part of her enthusiastic cleaning binge. Freaking Cinderella.

Well, at least it meant Liz didn't have to go to the trouble of making a new pot of coffee herself. She set her empty cup in the sink with a sigh.

"Don't tell me you're actually taking a break?" Jade said.

"More like the break is taking me. If I work on this dissertation another second I'm going to email Dr. Bennett and tell her what I really think of her."

"An honest, *calm* conversation might be good for both of you. But for now, why don't you come with me to the cat café? We're going to discuss the cat festival."

"There's a cat festival?"

Jade grinned. "It's in June, and they're hoping to bring in tourists."

"Sure, why not."

"Great, I'll be ready to leave in five." Jade danced off to her room.

Liz had actually meant *Sure, why not a cat festival to draw in tourists?*—spoken ironically, because *Huh?*—but whatever. The cat café would have coffee, and getting out of the house would keep her from sending an email she might regret.

They walked into town, since it was, according to Jade, a gorgeous spring day. Liz would have called it tolerably warm but unpleasantly windy. As they reached the cat café, Liz's gaze landed on the sign, which said the café would open at noon. After a moment's reflection, she decided it was indeed Sunday, and it couldn't yet be noon. But before she could speak, Jade was pulling open the door.

"I don't think they're open yet," Liz said.

"Just for the meeting."

"You didn't say I'd have to attend a meeting." Liz glared at the back of Jade's head but followed her inside. "Am I being volunteered for something?"

Jade paused in the hallway. "You know I'm going to take any chance I can to get you away from our house and your lab. You don't have to do anything, but maybe you'll enjoy meeting some people who aren't driving you crazy."

"Yeah, because I don't currently know *anyone* in that category," Liz grumbled. At least she smelled coffee.

Jade looked through the interior windows into the room with the cats. "Oh! Can you get me a latte?" She headed into the bigger room.

Liz ordered two lattes from the golden retriever barista—Dustin, per his nametag. They made small talk while he prepared the drinks. He really was cute, but way too perky. One person like that in Liz's life was plenty.

She took the drinks into the main room, where a dozen people stood around in noisy conversation. Liz squeezed in beside Jade and held out the drink.

Jade said, "Liz meet Cheyenne. She runs Big Cat Rescue!"

Good thing Liz hadn't started sipping coffee, or she might have choked on it. So this was Jade's nefarious plan. Liz had been avoiding the wild cat rescue and everyone who worked there, because getting involved now would only make her torturous PhD that much more unbearable. Yes, she knew she should be networking, but it was hard enough to buckle down to research when she didn't have the temptation of hanging out with wild animals and the people who loved them and wanted to save them.

Fortunately, Jade started explaining Liz's research, giving Liz time to mentally regroup. Plus it meant Liz didn't have to find a way to introduce the subject herself. Sometimes Jade wasn't half bad. Maybe Liz wouldn't kill her later.

A couple of minutes later, Jade left Liz to chat with Cheyenne.

"I hear Jade has applied for a grant to start a special needs branch of the domestic cat rescue," Cheyenne said.

"That's right. There's a local family ..." Liz trailed off, her brain warning her that she might have heard gossip about Cheyenne.

Cheyenne chuckled. "I know. My husband, Nash, helped start Big Cat Rescue."

"Nash ... The guy Jade met with was named Carl."

"Right, Carl and Nash run the family's charitable foundation. It got to be too much for one person to handle."

Must be nice, having so much money you needed help giving part of it away. Since Liz couldn't exactly make that comment out loud, she said, "I guess you're all cat lovers."

"Well, more or less. Nash actually used to have a phobia, but he got treatment."

"Really?" Liz had heard of cat phobia but never met anybody with it. "Hey, maybe that's what was wrong with Will. Although he didn't seem scared so much as disgusted by being around so many cats. I guess *he* won't be here today."

"Will?"

"You'd remember if he ever came to Big Cat Rescue, which I can't imagine happening. He'd probably be like—" Liz cringed like a cartoon elephant seeing a mouse.

Then it hit her: Cheyenne was living with Nash, and Nash used to have a cat phobia. Liz's attempt at humor might not land well.

She tried to backtrack. "Because of the fur and smell and, uh, stuff. William struck me as a man who wouldn't want to get his expensive shoes dirty or risk a claw snagging his suit."

"Hm." Cheyenne nodded past Liz's shoulder. "That wouldn't be him now, would it?"

Liz swung around in horror as Carl came through the

door with William and Caroline trailing behind. Liz gulped. He couldn't have heard her. Right? That group must have still been on the café side of the windows when she'd spoken. But how well did sound carry between the rooms? She could certainly hear the espresso maker through the window, but those machines were loud. And Liz had been facing away from the window. So she was fine. Probably.

She tried to will the heat out of her face as she turned back to Cheyenne. "Whoops."

"Mm." Fortunately, Cheyenne looked more amused than annoyed.

Still, Liz didn't want to slink away with her tail between her legs—which, come to think of it, was more of a dog thing than a cat thing, since cats never admitted wrongdoing. Anyway, if Liz ever finished her PhD she might want to volunteer at Big Cat Rescue for the experience, and if she walked away from Cheyenne now, she'd never have the nerve to show her face again.

"I should apologize," Liz said. "I've been cranky all week, and I wasn't expecting a big meeting when Jade invited me to the café ... Never mind all that. I shouldn't have been rude."

Cheyenne gave her arm a quick pat. "It happens to the best of us. I'm not the one who deserves the apology, but I don't think he heard you, so maybe it's best not to say anything to William."

Liz winced. "Yeah, I don't want to apologize for insulting him and then have to explain *how* I insulted him."

"Maybe he deserves a second chance though?"

Liz didn't want to give William a second chance. She didn't want to see him. She wanted to take her latte and go home. But more work awaited her at home, and Liz did have manners, even if she didn't always remember them, and she didn't want to risk Jade losing the funding if Liz's blunder offended Carl's friends.

She forced herself to smile. "Of course. It was nice to meet you."

"You, too." Cheyenne maneuvered through the crowd to join a tall man with dark hair going silver at the temples. They smiled at each other and shared a quick kiss before finding seats.

Kari, the café owner, was nudging people to settle down and be quiet. Carl joined Jade and the two stood close together, all smiles. Caroline found a chair near her brother. William backed away from the group. He glanced at Liz, one of the few people still standing, and gave a brief nod with an awkward half smile. Before she could force her face into an equally awkward smile, he headed for the hallway. Oh, drat! He was leaving already.

He sat at the counter on the other side of the windows.

Oh, drat. She had no excuse now.

Liz could take an empty seat and fake interest in the meeting. That would be a way to avoid William a little longer. Or she could slip out of the café and waste a precious weekend day pounding her head against her dissertation.

Or she could woman up and make nice with the annoying cat hater, for Jade's sake and her own reputation.

She sighed and headed after him.

Chapter 4

William had taken two types of allergy medicine this time. That was the good news. Or at least partly good news. He knew the pills helped when he was around one or two cats for the day. Fifteen or twenty? That might be another issue. But at least the café staff cleaned more often than some cat-owning people he knew.

The bad news was that he felt awkward and out of place as they entered the main café room. Carl had assured William he'd be welcome to hang out during the meeting, but William was wary about getting trapped into volunteering for something if he took too much interest. He wasn't absolutely opposed to volunteering, but he preferred to have time to think about it and make a rational decision rather than be put on the spot.

In fact, one reason he'd agreed to come along was to make sure Caroline didn't volunteer the two of them for something that would force him into her company even more. So he had to keep an eye on the meeting but didn't want to seem like an eager volunteer ready to take any task assigned, which was a tricky balance.

Most people were standing around and chatting. William wasn't sure what to do with himself. He spotted the boy he'd asked to help Caroline with her pictures on the last visit. The kid grinned and waved.

"Look, Brian's here," William told Caroline. Maybe he could get her distracted by social media opportunities again.

Caroline aimed a beauty pageant smile in the boy's direction and waved. Then she muttered to William, "He has such a crush on me. It's terribly awkward when he's so much younger."

"Must be tough," William said dryly.

"Oh, no, he's coming this way." Caroline turned toward William and would have brushed his chest with hers if he hadn't stepped back. "Poor boy," she said. "I hate to be rude, but I wouldn't want to lead him on. Let's make it clear I'm not available." She giggled.

"Maybe you'll be lucky and he'll notice your obvious disinterest." William couldn't back up any farther because people were behind him. He gazed over Caroline's head to avoid making the moment more intimate. The boy darted sideways and ducked down. He emerged from the crowd a moment later holding the fluffy cat that looked like a perfectly toasted marshmallow.

Brian walked toward them holding the cat to his chest. William smiled at him.

"Hi! I'm putting Lydia in the office so she doesn't get stepped on. She's a little too friendly sometimes." Brian headed out the door.

"I guess you're safe," William told Caroline. He squeezed sideways through the group. "You'd better grab a seat. I'm going to ..." He waved vaguely toward the window that led to the café area. They already had their coffee or tea, but maybe she'd think he was going to get pastries or use the restroom.

"I'll save you a seat!" she said.

"No need." He waited until she was seated and then escaped to the hallway. It had the café serving counter on one side and a long row of windows between the food area and the cat room opposite it. Maybe he'd park himself in one of these seats and hope he could figure out what was going on in the meeting quickly enough to head off any problems.

He should have skipped the whole thing and tasked Carl to keep him out of it all.

And yet ... The other reason he'd agreed to come followed him out the door and turned toward him. He'd been intrigued by his brief chat with Liz. Cynical, snarky women—what could he say? Not to mention she had fantastic eyes. He'd always been a sucker for beautiful eyes, almost as much as for an irreverent attitude. She was edging closer with a smile on her lips but a look in those fine eyes that said she'd be happy to chew him up, spit him out, and walk away without a backward glance, and he'd probably enjoy it. Okay, that last part might be his interpretation, not hers. Possibly he had some submission fantasies he should ponder sometime, but he couldn't think about that now.

"Hello again," she said.

"Hi." Her eyes were even better up close, a rich brown like sunlight on mahogany.

He dragged his gaze away so he wouldn't stare and pretended to watch a gray cat sleeping in a hammock on the other side of the windows. He checked that it wasn't doing anything lewd. It was safely wrapped in a pretzel shape with one leg shooting out of the jumble.

He cleared his throat. "Nice to see you again."

She gave a derisive little snort and then turned it into a cough. "Yeah. Um. You, too."

He couldn't think of a single thing to say.

She sipped her drink. "So. You're here for the volunteer meeting?"

"Not exactly. I'm here to make sure I don't get volunteered for something I don't want to do." Wait, did that sound like he didn't think the cause was worth his time? "I mean, they're welcome to the money, but I'm protective of my time."

"What money?"

"What?"

She didn't roll her eyes, but he thought she wanted to. "You said they're welcome to the money. *What* money?"

"Whatever money they need to fund this festival."

"How generous," she said. "Whose money are we talking about?"

"Well, the Anderson family charitable fund would supply the donation, or I suppose a loan to businesses that need some cash upfront to fund whatever it is they want to do for the festival, if they expect to make money in return."

Her eyebrows drew together. "I thought you didn't work with Carl on the charity stuff."

"I don't." He felt like they were running through a comedy routine, like *Who's on first?*, but he hadn't yet figured out where they'd gone wrong.

Her foot tapped the floor. "Then it's a bit disingenuous for you to say they can have the money, isn't it?"

"Oh. I see. Yes, or rather no, I'm not the one who decides. I'm in the financial department of Anderson Technology."

"Oh, so you do work for the Anderson family."

"Well, sort of."

"What does that mean?" She looked increasingly frustrated.

"I'm a member of the Anderson family." He gestured toward the volunteer group. "Nash is my cousin. He runs the charitable arm. I help make sure we have money coming in for them to give away."

She froze, eyes wide and mouth slightly open. He'd assumed she knew who he was. Small town gossip and all. So much for his ego.

"You didn't know?" He steeled himself for her reaction, hoping she wouldn't turn fawning and flattering. He had enough of that in his life. He'd been impressed because she'd treated him like a regular person instead of a potential rich husband, sugar daddy, or naïve investor in some get-rich-quick scheme. Apparently that was because she thought he *was* a regular person—which he was, except for the family connection. He almost wished he hadn't explained, but he had a hard enough time communicating without trying to keep track of secrets.

She propped one hand on her hip. "No, I've been hiding under the rock of my PhD dissertation. I didn't have time to keep up my scrapbook of local royalty."

Oh, good, still snarky. He mentally scrambled for a new topic. The only things he knew about her—she was a PhD student, and she occasionally visited the cat café—

seemed fraught with the potential to offend. But he would not default to the banality of the weather. He chose the lesser of the apparent conversational evils.

"How is your dissertation going?"

She groaned loudly and slapped her hand over her eyes.

William blinked at her. Now what had he said? He glanced back at the two baristas, but they were deep in conversation and apparently hadn't noticed Liz's reaction. In the main room, Caroline was twisted around frowning at William and Liz, but she probably couldn't hear them.

"Um. Sorry?" He wasn't sure why he was apologizing, but apparently he'd chosen the wrong option again.

She dropped her hand and scowled. "The number one rule for dealing with PhD students is *Do not ask how their dissertation is going*! Because the answer is always that it's going terribly."

"Sorry." Come to think of it, that explained the PhDs who put such excessive value on their degrees. If they'd suffered that much to get one, they probably needed it to matter a lot.

She took a deep breath and let it out. "It's okay. I shouldn't have groaned at you."

He smiled cautiously. "Is it safe to ask what your dissertation is about, or at least what field you're studying?"

Her grin lit up her face like someone had turned a spotlight on it. "Yes, but only if you're excited about getting an hour-long lecture peppered with complaints."

If she kept smiling like that, he wouldn't mind listening to her for an hour.

Unfortunately, the smile dropped away quickly. "The short answer is, I'm studying animal intelligence. Specifically, worms, in case you were going to assume something more glamorous, like Jane Goodall and the chimpanzees."

He considered that. "Worm intelligence might be

interesting, I suppose. I admit I've never thought about it in any depth. Are worms intelligent?"

"Compared to humans, chimpanzees, or even chickens, no. Compared to bacteria, yes. Scientists are doing interesting work regarding brain structure mapping—and I'm going to stop before your eyes glaze over."

"I'm interested."

She scoffed. "Yeah, right. In any case, I came here to get away from my dissertation, so let's skip it."

"If you like. Then … can I ask how you got into worms?"

The grin flashed again, there and gone. "That sounds utterly disgusting. I spend some time in the lab, but most of my work is done on the computer, working with data we've already collected. I guess I should be grateful I'm not hip-deep in worms on a daily basis."

"That would be … a lot of worms."

"Anyway, I started in biology. That's how I met my roommate, Jade." She bobbed her head toward the volunteer group. "She wanted to be a vet, but she didn't get into vet school—it's really competitive, only one in five applicants are accepted—so after we got our bachelor's degrees, she started working at the cat rescue to get more animal experience for the next time she applied. Then she decided she liked it there. I went on to graduate school, to my everlasting regret."

"I imagine you didn't graduate high school with a deep desire to study worms," he said.

She narrowed her gaze. "What if I did?"

Shoot, he'd misjudged again. "Oh, that's cool. Um, not many teens—"

"I'm kidding. I actually wanted to be another Jane Goodall. Too many people do." A marmalade cat squeezed into the hammock next to the gray cat. Liz lightly tapped her finger across the glass and the cat batted back at them. "Life had other plans."

"But you're still there. In grad school, I mean. You must be ..." If he suggested she was enjoying it, she'd probably scoff again. "You must have a reason for staying. Something you're getting out of it."

Her lips twisted. She kept her gaze on the cats. "Sometimes I wonder."

"Presumably no one is holding a gun to your head." He tried to lighten the mood, hoping to see that smile again. "Blink twice if you're being forced to complete a dissertation against your will."

Her laugh sounded reluctant. "More like I'm being forced to *not* complete a dissertation against my will."

He tried to figure out that meaning.

Before he got very far, she gave a quick shake of her head. "Never mind. I'm sure you're not interested in my dissertation delays and they're certainly not your problem." She glanced toward the volunteer group. "I know I'm whining when I'm envious of Jade, who also makes next to nothing working long hours, but she does it at a job that involves *literal* poop, plus blood and pus and falling in love with sick and injured animals that, best case scenario, you fix up and give away to other people."

That was a lot to process. He hadn't thought about animal rescue in those terms. Plenty of people thought it sounded wonderful to work with animals, but it must be an exhausting, heartbreaking job with low pay. William had grown up with strong family values about helping those in need and giving back to the community. All the cousins were expected to go to college and start careers; they didn't get huge trust funds. Still, William had never worried about money. He knew lots of people did, and he understood that many people were not technically "living in poverty" but still struggled to pay unexpected bills at times.

He hadn't realized pretty, cheerful Jade or tough, no-nonsense Liz might be in that category. Maybe he still had things to learn.

And he'd been silent for far too long. He scrambled for something to say. "I guess you don't make deep personal connections with the worms."

She chuckled. "They're pretty good listeners, since they don't interrupt or talk back. And I don't get their bodily fluids all over me. So." She shrugged. "Yay, me? And before you can say it, I know I should count my blessings, other people have it worse, etcetera."

"I wasn't going to say that." Comparative suffering was pointless. He had money, but that didn't save him from social anxiety. He had family members who would probably trade their fortune in return for a cure for their physical or mental illnesses, if they had that choice. It seemed like everyone faced some kind of trial: physical, mental, financial, or familial. If you were lucky, you only had one challenge.

"Okay." She sipped coffee and glanced around as if looking for something more interesting.

He spoke quickly to keep the conversation going a little longer. "You never said why you stayed in grad school if you dislike it so much."

Her face scrunched up and she didn't say anything for a while. He stayed quiet so he wouldn't interrupt her thinking.

Finally she said, "A lot of reasons. I want the job opportunities the degree could provide. I don't want to be a quitter. I've been doing this so long—it kind of feels like changing course would be like trying to turn the Titanic."

"Er..."

"Yeah, I recognize the problem with that metaphor. Anyway, my parents both have PhDs. I'm officially the first generation that can't be more educated than my parents, unless I get multiple PhDs, and that is not going to happen."

"Huh." He understood something about parental pressure. "Do you want to be more educated than them? Do they expect you to be?"

"Maybe not more, but if I don't get my PhD I'm going to hear about it during every family visit ever." Her shrug looked like she was trying to throw something off her shoulders. "That's enough about me. Anything you want to share?"

Open-ended questions were the worst. He couldn't think of anything interesting to tell her about himself. He was good with numbers, he'd studied accounting, and he spent most of the time on a computer tracking accounts and preparing reports. Most people thought that was boring. It certainly wasn't anything fascinating and potentially world changing like understanding animal intelligence. If he told her he was the lead financial manager for a multi-million-dollar company, at best, she'd think he was bragging, and at worst, she'd think he was boring *and* bragging.

What else? He liked playing tabletop games, both board games and cards. That probably sounded boring as well. He liked taking long walks and sometimes hikes, and lately he'd been trying to take time-lapse night sky pictures. That was starting to sound too much like a dating profile—"long walks and looking at the stars."

"I have a dog," he finally said.

Her mouth worked in an expression he couldn't decipher. "Of course you do."

Chapter 5

Finally Kari got everyone settled down and called the meeting to order, giving Liz an excuse to join the main group. She even managed to dodge all the big work assignments, since she had so little free time, though she did agree to help at registration on the day of the parade. A cat parade. That should be interesting.

The meeting wrapped up as the café opened. It was crowded for a few minutes as customers came in while some of the volunteers left and others grabbed drinks or snacks. William left with Carl and Caroline, Cheyenne passed Liz a business card and walked out with Nash, and finally Liz could relax with another coffee and a giant cat-shaped cookie.

Jade was practically dancing as she waved a feather wand for two of the kittens to chase. Carl had, apparently, basically promised her the donation she needed.

"I saw you talking with William," Jade said. "He's nice, right?"

Liz huffed out a laugh. "Sure. When I went up to him, he looked at me for about two seconds and then stared at one of the cats as he said, 'Nice to see you again.' He couldn't make it more obvious that I'm less interesting than cats, and we know how he feels about cats."

"He's probably just shy. I can't imagine Carl would be such good friends with him if William wasn't a great guy. Caroline obviously likes him too."

"Obviously."

Jade either missed Liz's implication or chose to ignore it. She twitched the stick for the kittens. The feathers on the end jumped as the kittens tried to catch them. The calico tumbled over the black kitten and got up facing the wrong way. The calico looked around, confused, until the feather bundle tapped her backside. She swung around and pounced, biting the plastic that held the feathers together.

"She's sweet, isn't she?" Jade said.

"The kitten?" Liz asked.

"No, Caroline! Well, obviously the kittens are sweet too."

The black kitten tackled the calico and the feather wand escaped as the two of them wrestled.

"The kittens are adorable little monsters, but *sweet* wasn't the word that came to mind with Caroline. Granted, she's young." Liz wasn't sure that was an excuse, but at least Caroline had plenty of time to change. Not that anyone would call Liz sweet either, and she had no intention of trying to be sweeter.

"You're so judgmental," Jade said mildly as she put the stick back in the enormous ceramic pot used to hold cat toys. She sank down on the bench next to Liz. "I like them."

Liz bumped Jade's shoulder with her own. "You like everyone. It's why you put up with me."

"At least you recognize that." Jade broke off a piece of Liz's cookie.

"Okay, maybe *that's* why you put up with me, thief."

Jade grinned and popped the cookie cat's ear into her mouth. The cookies were cute but kind of gruesome if you thought about it.

"I really do think they're nice though," Jade said. "Carl could have just made the donation, or refused it, and left things at that. Instead he's here to help plan the festival, and William and Caroline came along. How is that anything but nice?"

"Caroline came because William would be here, and she's crushing on him." Liz had no idea why William had come. Maybe he wanted to keep Carl from giving away too much money.

"Well, I like them."

"You go ahead and do that." Liz bumped Jade's shoulder again. "You've liked plenty of worse people. And I guess if you're going to hang out with Carl, you'll have to put up with his sister and best friend.”

Jade’s cheeks went pink. “It’s just business. Or charity. Both, I guess.”

“Maybe it started that way, but I see how he looks at you—and how you look at him, so there’s no point in denying it. It’s great. Just don’t try to foist William on me.”

“You could do worse,” Jade said.

“That’s not a high bar. Granted, he doesn’t hunt humans for fun or have a bizarre fetish—as far as we know.”

“Excuse me.” The voice came from Liz’s other side.

Oops. Apparently she still hadn’t learned to say nothing if she couldn’t say anything nice. Forget the PhD— she needed to go back to kindergarten.

She turned to see a man about their age with dark blond hair in a ponytail and a friendly smile. The fluffy cat, Lydia, was on his lap rubbing her face against his chest. She might have been drooling.

“I hope you’ll forgive me,” he said. “I didn’t mean to eavesdrop, but I saw William come out as I neared the café. It sounds like you’ve met him.”

Jade leaned forward to see past Liz. “Oh, you know him? Tell Liz there’s nothing wrong with him.”

“Hi, Liz.” The man held out his hand. “I’m George Wickham.”

Liz shook his hand, trying to decide whether she was annoyed at the interruption. On the one hand, she simply wanted to hang out with Jade and some cats. On the other hand, he had a firm grip, a decent smile, and gray eyes that seemed made for laughter. He wore a red jacket with gold trim. Kind of flashy, but it fit him well.

Jade leaned across Liz and held out her hand. “George? I’m Jade.”

He shook her hand. “As much as I wish I could comply with your request, I’m afraid I don’t have anything good to say about old Will.”

Okay, apparently they were going to have a conversation. At least Liz had an ally for her opinion. "See?" she told Jade. "Sometimes first impressions are the right ones."

"Hm. How long have you known William?" Jade asked George.

"Practically all our lives. We grew up in the same neighborhood and were in the same grade. He was weird even then."

"There's nothing wrong with weird," Jade said. "It's usually better than normal."

George shrugged. "I guess it depends on the type of weird. I don't like to criticize anyone, but watch yourself around William."

Liz frowned. She didn't want to encourage gossip, but a statement like that demanded clarification. If William did hunt humans for fun, they ought to know about it. "Watch ourselves how?"

George looked down at Lydia and rubbed behind her ears. "I'm not saying he's dangerous, exactly. Just a little unpredictable. And his dog." He shuddered. "Now there's a vicious beast. And you know what they say, a dog's behavior reflects his owner."

"Are you saying he mistreats the dog?" Liz's stomach churned. She hadn't gotten that impression from William, but she barely knew him. Plenty of dogs were poorly trained and rambunctious, but *vicious* implied a mean streak, and that often came from abuse. "If it's an animal cruelty situation ..."

"I wouldn't go that far. It's more that he doesn't properly control the dog." George wrapped one arm around Lydia to hold her in place as he leaned forward. He pulled up his jeans to show his calf. "That's how I got this scar."

The side of his right calf had a white patch as big as Liz's palm. She stared for a few seconds before raising her gaze to George's. "His dog bit you? Did you report that?"

He dropped his pants leg and shook his head. "Like I said, it's not the dog's fault, and I didn't want the poor animal to be put down."

"But if it's a hazard to the public ..." Liz hated the idea of a healthy dog being euthanized, but dangerous dogs couldn't be let loose to injure people. What if it got a hold of a child?

"He promised to keep his dog confined or on a leash," George said. "I don't have any evidence that he's broken that promise."

Jade looked upset. "Accidents do happen. That sounds really scary, but I'm glad you worked things out with William."

"We basically agreed to avoid each other." A muscle in George's jaw clenched. "I give him a wide berth and suggest you do the same."

"That works for me," Liz said. "I take it you're a cat lover."

George grinned. "There's something wrong with people who don't like cats. I know some people say cats are standoffish, but come on, look at this." Lydia was rubbing her head against his neck and making little chirping sounds. "We just met and she acts like I'm her long-lost best friend."

"All the cats here are available for adoption," Jade said. "You could apply to take her home."

"Yeah, maybe I will. What was going on here before the place opened today?"

Jade explained about the volunteer meeting. After that they somehow got onto the topic of Liz's research. George was easy to talk to and clearly interested in what she had to say. He didn't even joke about her worms. Liz hadn't had such a relaxing weekend in years.

"We'd better go." Jade glanced at the window, where large drops of rain were starting to splatter the glass. "So much for the storm coming in this evening."

"Yeah, I need to go too," George said. "I work pretty

long hours during the week, so Sunday is my day to catch up on chores."

By the time they gathered their things and headed for the door, the wind was whipping sheets of rain against the windows.

"So much for walking because it's a nice day," Liz said. "I guess we're going to get wet on the way home."

"Let me drop you off," George offered.

Liz glanced at Jade, who shrugged.

"Yeah, okay," Liz said. "Thanks."

Normally she wouldn't accept a ride with someone she'd just met, and she wouldn't want him to know where she lived. But they'd chatted for an hour and George seemed like a great guy. Besides, Liz and Jade would be together. And even more to the point, the temperature had dropped ten degrees since they'd walked over that morning.

"Great." George winked. "That gives me time to wheedle your phone number from you and maybe even ask for a date."

Liz chuckled. She did like confidence, so much so that she gave him her phone number as they pulled up to their apartment building, although she refused to commit to a date. He could follow up if he was that determined.

They still got wet running from the car to the front door, but at least they weren't soaked. Inside, Liz ran her fingers through her hair to flick away the water. "Well, that was fun but a longer break than I was planning. I'd better get back to work."

Jade was looking at her phone. "Uh-oh. The power went out at the rescue. I'd better get over there to help."

"Yikes. Do you need me?"

"No, I know you're anxious to get back to your dissertation. Make sure you're backing up your work every few minutes in case we lose power here too!" Jade grabbed her car keys and a raincoat and headed out.

Liz tried to settle down to work, but her mind kept

drifting. She now had a contact at Big Cat Rescue. Could she afford the time to volunteer there? She'd liked Cheyenne and it would be cool to work with lions and tigers, animals that were about as different from worms as possible. But she already worked too hard, and her dissertation had to be her priority.

She shouldn't even think about dating. George was fun, and she needed more fun in her life, but she didn't have the time to commit to a relationship until the dreaded dissertation was done. Maybe he'd accept an occasional night out and understand if she basically ignored him in between.

George and William were definitely opposites, almost as much opposites as worms and big cats. Liz had tried giving William a second chance, and it had gone only slightly better than the first meeting. She'd be polite, for Jade and Carl's sake, but men like that were too much work.

The lights flickered. Liz quickly hit save on her document. She wasn't getting anything done, so she might as well shut down the computer and then microwave some dinner before they lost power entirely.

The storm raged outside, rain lashing the windows. Lightning flashed, followed moments later by thunder. The power flickered a few more times. Good thing they had backup generators at the lab. Liz could go there to work—but she didn't want to go out in the storm. Better to go to bed early so she could get an early start in the morning.

Sausage, their current foster cat, meowed and headbutted her ankles. He'd been dropped off at the rescue after his owner had died, because the heirs didn't want to deal with the overweight cat's health problems. With a better diet and gentle exercise, he'd lost five pounds and become more active. The gray striped tabby still looked like a sausage, or in Liz's opinion more like a baby seal, but he no longer limped from the arthritis caused by the extra weight on his tiny legs and feet, and he needed less medication.

"Okay, let's go to bed." Sausage preferentially slept on Jade's bed, but with Jade gone, maybe he'd keep Liz company.

She slept restlessly, dreaming of chasing giant house cats through a storm.

She woke in pitch blackness to a strange groaning, creaking sound. Liz lay in her bed, staring into the dark. What *was* that?

The groan turned to a rumble and then—*Crash!*

The bed shook. When it stopped moving, Liz scrambled out and stumbled into the hallway. "Jade?"

No answer. Jade's bedroom door was open. Liz peeked in, saw nothing in the dark, and flipped the light switch, praying it would work. The lights went on. She grabbed the doorframe, trembling with relief. Jade's bed was empty and neatly made, the way she left it every morning. Jade must still be at the cat rescue. A dip in the pillow suggested Sausage had been sleeping there. Had the cat knocked over something to cause such a crash?

Faint creaks, thumps, groans, and slithering sounds came from somewhere in the apartment. Liz checked the living room. It and the kitchen looked normal. She traced the sounds to the bathroom. When she turned on the lights, it took a minute to make sense of what she was seeing.

The ceiling had collapsed. The tub from the apartment above theirs was now sitting on a pile of rubble in their bathroom. Dust swirled, sending her coughing.

Her stomach dropped and her legs went weak. Voices drifted through the hole, so the noise must have awoken the upstairs neighbors and they had discovered the problem too, but no one was screaming. Jade was still at the rescue, right?

Yes, Liz had turned on the bathroom light. If Jade had come home and wanted a shower, she wouldn't have been showering in the dark. And no one from upstairs appeared to have plummeted into her bathroom along with the tub.

"Sausage!" Where was the cat?

"What?" someone called from upstairs.

Liz ignored him and hurried through the house until she found Sausage hiding under Jade's bed. He must have retreated there when the noise startled him. Liz coaxed him out and held him to her chest. She took a few seconds to simply breathe.

"Okay. You're fine. I'm fine. But neither of us are going into that bathroom." Liz found the pet carrying case in Jade's closet and put Sausage inside. She put the case by the front door and draped a fleece blanket over it to keep the cat warm and calm—or at least somewhat calmer, since Sausage didn't like confinement.

Liz rubbed her hands over her face and went back to her bedroom to grab her phone. It was 3 AM. She pulled on clothes and shoes, because she was shivering and would clearly not be going back to sleep anytime soon. She headed out to talk to the upstairs neighbors. They'd have to call the landlord, which would make one more person unhappy to be jolted awake at 3 AM.

Then what? Who knew how long repairs would take? How could they manage without a bathroom for days, maybe weeks?

This was not the early start she'd wanted.

Chapter 6

The guys upstairs said their ceiling was fine, oddly enough. However, the tiles on their bathroom wall had been bowing inward for months, which they had not bothered to report to anyone. Liz resisted yelling at them for that, since it was too late, and if they hadn't yet recognized their poor judgment, nothing she could say would make them. Also, the landlord would probably take care of the yelling.

The guys headed to the roof in the pouring rain to investigate, while Liz woke everyone else in the building and explained why she was pounding on their door at that hour.

Hank and Fred reported no visible roof collapse, but there was a six-inch deep puddle in the corner above their bathroom. They theorized that water from the wet winter had been pooling on the roof and slowly leaking down inside the wall for months.

Then another neighbor mentioned the word "condemned." Once the damage was reported, they might not be allowed back in the building even to retrieve their belongings. Liz grabbed Sausage and extra blankets, while the neighbors evacuated their pets. Mrs. Aguilar called her daughter and son-in-law to pick up all the animals and give them shelter for the night, so that made two more people enjoying the fun.

Over the next few hours, Liz got increasingly wet as she carried loads out to the car, starting with their electronic devices. She had never been so grateful to live in the modern era of digital media where most things were stored in the cloud. Liz was able to carry all their computer stuff in one trip. What if they'd had those ancient, heavy computer monitors?

Of course, Hank and Fred staggered downstairs carrying a giant flat screen TV between them. Not everything had been condensed.

Then Liz packed suitcases full of clothes for herself and Jade. She couldn't enter the bathroom, so the toiletries, makeup, and medicines would have to be replaced. She couldn't move the furniture, and it would take too long to pack up the dishes, silverware, towels, linens and so forth. Besides, the car was already full, and she didn't know where she'd take the things she'd already rescued. Would they lose everything they had to leave behind? It was only stuff, but it must add up to thousands of dollars' worth of stuff, accumulated over years, and neither she nor Jade had thousands of dollars to replace it all.

She couldn't think about that yet.

The rain slowed to a drizzle as gray dawn filtered through the windows. Liz stood in the living room looking at all the remaining stuff. Should she try to retrieve the framed photos and posters from the walls? The spider plants in hanging baskets? She was shaky and queasy and chilled. She wanted to crawl in bed under a pile of blankets. But she had no idea when she'd have a chance to sleep, let alone where.

It was just stuff. They'd had no loss of life, human or pet.

It was still hard to feel lucky.

Footsteps came quickly down the building hallway. Liz turned toward the door she'd left open. Jade appeared in the doorway and they stared at each other. Liz hadn't called her, figuring the rescue might need Jade more than Liz did. But at the sight of her best friend, tears filled her eyes.

Then they were embracing. "You're all right," Jade whispered. "Mrs. Aguilar said so, but ..."

"I'm fine." It felt like a lie. "Our bathroom is definitely not. I think I got the most important things—oh, your asthma medicine! You can't go into the bathroom, even if you could find anything in there ..."

"I have an inhaler on me. It will last until I can get the

prescription replaced." Jade gave a last squeeze and eased back. "I'm sorry you had to deal with all this alone."

"I imagine your night wasn't much better." Liz sighed. "Is there anything else we need if we can't get back in here for an undetermined amount of time?" She didn't want to say *ever*.

Jade wrinkled her nose. "I hate to think what the fridge will smell like when we get back, especially if they turn off the electricity to make repairs."

"Good point." They drank the last of the milk and packed a couple of canvas totes with perishables. Neither brought up the question of where they were going to put perishables when they no longer had a kitchen.

Something buzzed faintly. Jade pulled out her phone. "Oh, it's Carl, wondering how we're doing after the storm."

Liz made a sound that was distantly related to a laugh. The milk was settling her hungry stomach but she was lightheaded with fatigue.

Jade frowned for a few seconds and then tapped the screen and dictated her reply. "What a night! The good news is, we now have a second bathtub. The bad news is it came through the bathroom ceiling."

Liz snickered.

Jade met her gaze with an expression of sympathy that told Liz the lighthearted message was for her sake as much as Carl's. "But we're fine." She hesitated and then tapped the screen. "I don't even know what else to say. I'm too tired to think right now."

Moments later, Jade's phone rang. She held it to her ear as they scanned the apartment one last time. "Oh, hi, Carl! Yes, we really are fine. No one was hurt. I guess that's the good thing about a bathroom ceiling collapse in the middle of the night."

She was quiet for a minute, listening. "I don't know. I was at the rescue all night and just got home. Liz packed up stuff for us—no, we're leaving the building now for the last time, I promise."

She hooked bags over her shoulders and made a shooing motion to Liz. Liz hoisted her bags and they headed downstairs.

"Yes, we're outside now," Jade said as they left the building. "Hang on." She set the phone on top of a grocery bag and swung the rear of her hatchback up.

Liz deposited her bags inside, took Jade's from her, and then sat under the open hatch. It provided some shelter from the drizzle. Not that Liz could get much more wet, but the rain was cold.

"Oh, well, thank you," Jade said into her phone. "That would be a big help, if you're sure—" She looked at Liz with her eyes wide and eyebrows up. "All right. Text me the address. Thank you so much." She stuck her phone back in her pocket.

"What has the amazing Carl done now?" Liz barely got the sentence out before she had to cover a yawn.

"He's invited us to stay with him."

They stared at each other.

"That is ... remarkably nice," Liz said slowly.

"You see? Things tend to work out if you keep a positive attitude." Jade smiled beatifically.

Liz sighed. "Oh, Cinderella."

"What?"

"Nothing. In fact, things are probably working out because of your positive attitude."

Jade made friends easily and helped other people whenever she could. Sometimes people took advantage, but sometimes they rushed to do favors for Jade because she was so sweet. So of course a guy she'd met a week ago was inviting her into his home. Liz tried to imagine William's reaction to their plight. He probably wouldn't be happy they were suffering, but that was the best she could say, which was Liz's fault as much as William's.

Jade shrugged. "And he did say both of us, in case you're wondering. He said they have plenty of room."

"They?"

"Caroline lives with him."

"Of course she does." At least it wasn't William. Liz felt like she ought to argue, but what else were they going to do? They didn't have the money for weeks at a hotel, and she couldn't think of any friends with extra bedrooms. Her parents lived over three hours away. Besides, she wasn't about to move back in with them as long as she had any other options. That left her car or the lab, neither of which would be remotely comfortable. "Okay, let's go."

"Really? You don't think it's weird that someone we barely know is offering us a place to stay? I mean, I don't—I told you he was super nice—but ..."

"But I'm usually the suspicious one looking for nefarious motives." Liz managed a smile. "I'm too tired to argue, and I doubt Carl has any major skullduggery planned."

Jade chuckled. "Nefarious skullduggery. Good band name."

"Too hard to spell." Liz could totally think of ulterior motives Carl might have, but if he was interested in Jade and Jade was interested in him, and it got them a place to stay for a while ... Well, they could always move out if he tried anything Jade didn't like. At least they'd have someplace to go right away. Did "plenty of room" mean plenty of beds?

Liz pushed herself upright and only staggered a little. "Okay, lead the way and I'll follow."

They drove to a house on the outskirts of town. The house was big, but not mansion big. The yard had large, leafy trees and a brick walkway that had buckled, suggesting the home was decades old.

Carl came out as they parked. He greeted them warmly and helped carry in their belongings, which they piled in the large front hall. Caroline appeared a few minutes later wrapped in her bathrobe, her hair tangled. She didn't look happy to see Jade and Liz, but once she heard what had happened, she shrieked and gasped as dramatically as if it had happened to her.

Liz started yawning as Caroline said for the third time, "Oh, you *poor* things! To lose everything and be *homeless*!" Jade was actually comforting Caroline rather than the other way around.

Carl touched Liz's arm. "Let me show you your room." He grabbed her suitcase from the front hall and escorted her to a guest bedroom. "Please make yourself at home. Jade will be next door, and the two of you will share this bathroom." He gestured across the hall. "I hope that's all right."

"If the ceiling isn't going to fall on us, it's fine."

He glanced upward with a look of alarm. "The roof is only five years old, but—"

"I'm kidding. Thank you for letting us stay here today."

"For as long as you want. I'm so sorry this happened to you." Carl frowned and shook his head. "Thank goodness you weren't injured. To think—But you look exhausted, so I'll shut up now."

He couldn't have said anything that would please Liz more. She closed the bedroom door, dropped her damp clothes on the floor, and crawled between the covers. It might have been the most comfortable bed she'd ever been in, though that could have been the exhaustion talking.

She woke hours later and spent half a minute blinking at her surroundings before she remembered everything that had happened. Well. They were guests in Carl and Caroline's house. Liz didn't particularly like being a guest. She liked doing her own thing on her own schedule. She didn't want to feel obligated to socialize with her hosts, or wonder whether they felt obligated to socialize with her when they'd rather be doing something else.

But she was warm and dry and thankful for that.

She put on a T-shirt and peeked out the door. Jade's door was closed. The house was quiet. Liz took a long, hot shower and wrapped herself in a fluffy towel to cross the hallway. The house was still silent. What time was it? And would it be rude to scrounge breakfast, or should she go out to get something?

She got dressed and tracked down her phone. It was almost eleven a.m. and she had a string of texts from Dr. Bennett demanding to know where she was and why she was late. Technically, Liz wasn't late, since she didn't have official work hours, but she was almost always in by eight.

She texted back: *We had to deal with storm damage. I'll be in around noon.*

The reply came: *Be here by 1130. We have a lunch meeting.*

That was news to Liz. She decided she didn't care enough to ask for details. She'd find out soon enough. She gathered the things she needed to take with her.

As she headed toward the front of the house, her nose twitched. The smell of coffee came from the kitchen. Liz veered in that direction, hoping it wasn't the ghost smell of a former pot of coffee that had already been emptied. Then she'd have to decide whether to try to figure out their coffee maker and wait for it, or wait until she got to campus and hope to find a last, burned cup of mediocre coffee in a break room somewhere.

She turned at the archway into the kitchen and spotted the pot on the counter opposite. Still half full!

She took two steps into the kitchen before she realized she wasn't alone. William sat at the kitchen table with a newspaper.

Chapter 7

He set the paper down, pushed his chair back and stood. "Hello."

"Hi." Liz wanted to ask what he was doing there, but the question seemed rude when she was a guest too. She couldn't think of anything else to say. Her brain must not have fully recovered from the exhausting night.

William took two steps toward her. "I'm glad you're all right."

"Thank you." Great, she'd won him over. He was glad she hadn't had a bathtub fall on her head. Pretty soon they'd be weaving each other friendship bracelets.

"Carl had to go to work," he said. "Um. He asked me to wait here until you got up and make sure you have everything you need."

"You didn't need to do that. I'm sure you have more important things to do." And she could have found the coffee all by herself. Look, there it was!

"It's fine." He looked around. "So there's coffee, if you drink it. Do you want breakfast?"

Liz felt laughter building up inside of her. The situation was so ridiculous. Last night she'd been trying to rescue her most precious items, such as they were, in a rainstorm, because she'd suddenly lost her housing. This morning she'd woken in an extremely comfortable guestroom in a fancy house, and now a rich guy who didn't even like her was offering to ... make her breakfast? Or was he planning to call his chef? Take her out for a fancy brunch?

"That's not necessary. I need to get to the lab right away." Liz's gaze lingered on the coffee pot. She would give a lot for a cup—but not if she had to sit with William in awkward silence while she drank it.

"There are travel mugs in the cupboard if you want to take some with you," he said.

"That's the nicest thing anyone has said to me this week."

That got a smile out of him, or at least a slight curve of the lips. He went to the cupboard and pulled out several large, insulated mugs.

She chose one and filled it. "Thanks. Okay, I'd better get going."

"I can give you a ride."

She stared at him. "Unless I've forgotten something significant about last night, my car is parked outside."

"Yes, but isn't it hard to park on campus? You said you were in a hurry."

"Yeah, but ..." Now he was offering to play chauffeur? It was tempting just for the amusement factor. "Don't you have to get to work?"

"I took the day off."

Liz didn't know how to react to that. Apparently her expression spoke for her, because he shrugged and added, "I have plenty of vacation time. It was nice to be lazy and read the whole paper."

She glanced at the section he'd set on top of the newspaper pile. "Checking all the sports scores?"

"I'd read everything else."

"Yeah, sounds like a great vacation day. Okay, I guess giving me a ride is not less interesting than your last choice of newspaper section. If you drop me off, I'm sure I can find a ride home."

"Or you can call me. Let me give you my number." He retrieved a card from his wallet, pulled open a drawer that had pens and other miscellany, and scribbled a number on the card. "That's my cell phone. Call or text anytime."

Liz's brain was not too sluggish to notice a few things. He knew where to find the pens, so he was a regular visitor. No surprise if he was good friends with Carl. He'd added his cell phone number, so it wasn't on his business card. That could suggest he normally kept it private—but he was giving it to her. Maybe Carl had leaned on him hard to be helpful. Or maybe William knew Liz didn't like him any more than he liked her, so she wouldn't abuse the privilege.

Also, he'd given her a business card rather than telling her his number to put in her phone. She wasn't sure how to interpret that. He was old-fashioned? He didn't expect her to call more than once, if that, so she wouldn't need a permanent record of his number?

These were probably the least important things she had to think about that day. She shoved the card in her back pocket. "All right, I'll grab my computer and we can get going."

He followed her to the front hallway, where they'd left the things they didn't need overnight. It looked like a neater arrangement than she remembered.

"It's a good thing you were able to save so much," he said. "Although it sounds dangerous. You know, in an emergency, you really should leave everything behind and get yourself to safety."

She leaned down to grab her computer bag, which meant he couldn't see her face, so she rolled her eyes. She resisted the urge to say, *Thanks, Dad.* Not that her father would've said that. He would have told her to make sure she got her research out and leave everything else behind, including—

She straightened. "Oh! I need to figure out what to do with Sausage."

William's eyebrows drew together. "Is it in the refrigerator? Carl said you brought food. If it's something that needs to be cooked soon—"

Liz couldn't hold back her laughter this time. "No, Sausage is our cat. Mrs. Aguilar called her daughter and son-in-law to take in all the pets from the building last night so we didn't have to leave them in our cars while we were loading up stuff. I'm sure they'll want people to claim their pets as soon as they have a place to stay ..."

She hadn't thought to ask Carl and Caroline about

bringing the cat. Maybe Jade had. Or Sausage could go back to the rescue, but the poor cat was probably already stressed, and that would be one more stressful change.

"How many pets are we talking about?" William asked.

"For the whole building? There are twelve apartments with a strict one pet per apartment rule, so most people don't have more than two or three animals."

He cocked his head. "Is that a joke?"

"No. We're just a bunch of rule breakers. Jade and I have had as many as six cats at one time. Granted, they were newborn kittens, so the total poundage was less than one average adult cat, let alone Sausage."

He frowned over that. "You didn't keep the kittens."

"Only until they were old enough to get through the night without bottles. Then they could go back to the rescue."

He nodded. "Good. Do you want me to pick up your cat?" He opened the front door and held it for her.

She thought about the question as they walked toward his car, which was at least ten years newer and five times fancier than hers. He didn't like cats. Yet she trusted him to retrieve Sausage if she asked. She wasn't sure why. Maybe because he was dull and grumpy, but not mean.

He opened the passenger door for her, which confirmed her assessment of *old-fashioned*. She didn't need that kind of chivalry. She knew some women appreciated what they called "good manners," but she was physically healthy and one step short of a PhD. She didn't need to be treated like someone who didn't know how doors worked.

She slid onto the leather seat. He got in the driver's side and started the car. The touchscreen display showed that each front seat had an individual seat warmer. The thought of Sausage in this luxury car, shedding and no doubt yowling throughout the trip, almost set off another round of laughter.

Once Liz had her amusement under control, she said,

"I'll let you know about Sausage. I need to get an address and make sure Jade asked Carl if it was okay."

"Carl won't mind."

"How about Caroline?"

He hesitated. Finally he said, "It's Carl's house. Caroline was in a sorority house, until … Well, she's only supposed to be living with Carl until she graduates."

"Maybe so, but if I'm going to stay there, I don't want to get on Caroline's bad side."

"She says she likes cats." He shot Liz a glance that looked … apologetic? Uncomfortable? "To be honest, she's probably bragging about how generous they were in taking you in. I wouldn't mention it, but you ought to know. In case anyone else says anything."

Liz thought about that for a minute as they drove out of the neighborhood. "You mean she'll make it sound like Jade and I are poor, penniless waifs who needed their charity?" That fit with Caroline's overblown sympathy during the night.

"I don't know. Maybe. Just watch out if she has her phone pointed at you. She posts a lot of videos on social media."

"And she might not ask first."

William shrugged. Okay, he didn't want to criticize Caroline, but the message seemed clear enough.

"Thanks for the warning." She'd have to figure out how to handle that. She didn't need any negative publicity while she was finishing her dissertation and looking for work. Jade wouldn't want people to know she'd been forced out of her apartment either, not when she was trying to get funding for the special needs cat rescue. Liz didn't think their situation was shameful, but people were odd. Some might assume Liz was unreliable if she didn't have a permanent address at the moment, or they might think Jade would try to take the money for her own needs. Liz would have to find a way to shut down Caroline's desire for social media attention without offending her so much it got Carl upset and he kicked them out or backed out of funding Jade's rescue.

She leaned back and sighed. It was going to be a long week.

During the short drive, Liz called Ms. Aguilar. That also allowed her to avoid conversation with William. When Mrs. Aguilar rattled off the address, Liz said, "Uh, hang on" and looked around for someplace to write a note. William tapped the display screen and brought up the GPS. Okay, he wasn't entirely old-fashioned. She put the address in it and said goodbye to Mrs. Aguilar.

"All right, someone will be there all day. A few people have picked up their pets, but I guess a lot of us haven't figured out our plans yet. They'll be delighted to reduce the number of animals in their house. If you're sure Carl won't mind."

"If he does, I'll keep your cat at my house."

He must be really confident that Carl wouldn't mind. That made Liz feel a little better. Poor Sausage had gone through enough and would do better in a quiet house. Liz or Jade could keep him in one of their rooms if necessary. She remembered the plush carpet. Okay, maybe the bathroom. It had plenty of room for a litter box, food and water dishes, and some blankets. The thought of leaving a living creature in a bathroom made her cringe now. The chances of another ceiling collapse were slim, but it might take a while for her to feel entirely at ease again.

They reached campus and she directed him toward her building. He pulled up as close as one could get and said, "I'd like to see your lab."

"Really? I got you that excited about worms, huh?"

He had a smile if you looked closely enough. "I'm more interested in your research, but I don't have anything against worms. Well, at least not in a lab. They do good work in the garden as well. I don't want worms in my dog—or myself, for that matter, but I assume the worms don't attack everyone who comes in the lab."

"I'd be in trouble if they did. Attack of the Killer Worms? Now there's a horror movie."

He chuckled. He couldn't really be that interested. Maybe Carl had insisted William be friendly to Liz, the same way Jade wanted Liz to be friendly to William. Or maybe Jade had asked William to keep an eye on Liz and make sure she was okay after the stress of the night before. If Liz put off William's request now, he probably wouldn't ask again.

"Apparently my advisor has us scheduled for a lunch meeting with someone important, so today's not good for a visit. And I really have to run, but thanks for the ride!" She grabbed her bag and opened the car door.

"Call me when you're ready to be picked up," he said.

"Yeah. Sure." She escaped the car and headed for the lab.

Chapter 8

Liz got to the lab, dropped off her computer bag, and found her advisor.

"There you are! It's about time." Dr. Bennett frowned at Liz's clothes. "You ought to have worn something more professional."

Liz wasn't sure she had professional clothes. "I always wear jeans and a T-shirt in the lab. Besides, we had to evacuate our apartment in the middle of the night. All my clothes got jammed into a suitcase. At least jeans don't show wrinkles."

Dr. Bennett checked her watch. "I suppose it's too late to do anything about it now. This is an important opportunity for you. Dr. Collins has a postdoc available and I persuaded him to consider you."

Liz went lightheaded. "Does that mean you're going to approve my dissertation?"

"The postdoc starts in the fall, so you'll have all summer to finish it. If you buckle down and work night and day, you can manage it."

"Right." Liz held in a sigh and reminded herself that she had chosen to work with Dr. Bennett. There weren't a lot of women research professors in her field, so Liz had grabbed the opportunity, assuming she'd have someone sympathetic to guide her and would avoid some of the sexism still rampant in the sciences.

She'd overlooked the fact that Dr. Bennett was from a different generation—one where women basically gave up their personal lives in order to be successful. She had no children, and her relationship with her husband seemed distantly cordial. She had professional colleagues but few friends. She'd never mentioned a hobby. And instead of working to make things better for the younger generation, Dr. Bennett expected her underlings to make the same sacrifices she'd had to make.

What was the point of breaking new ground if

everyone behind you had to struggle with the same hard soil?

But at least Dr. Bennett was trying to get Liz a postdoc. That had to count for something, right?

"Is there anything I should know about Dr. Collins?" Liz asked.

"He's pompous and talks too much, but he has twice the budget we do." Dr. Bennett glanced around—they were alone—and then gave Liz a stern look. "You will be able to fill me in on any interesting research they are doing."

Liz tried to keep her face blank. It figured that this meeting was for Dr. Bennett's sake rather than Liz's. The woman expected Liz to be so loyal she'd spy on her next employer for her dissertation advisor's sake. That wouldn't happen. Once Liz had her PhD, the only thing they'd see of her was the dust she kicked up as she raced away. She'd probably run into Dr. Bennett again at conferences and so forth, given the relatively small size of their community. But playing some kind of double agent was out of the question.

Maybe she should be principled enough to tell Dr. Bennett that now. But keeping quiet might be the only way Liz would get her dissertation approved by the end of summer.

Dr. Bennett glanced at her watch. "Let's go. You can drive."

"I don't have a car here. A friend dropped me off." How odd to call William a friend, but it sounded better than saying, "Someone I barely know and don't much like gave me a ride."

Dr. Bennett huffed in annoyance. "Fine, I'll drive. I'll have to give up my good parking spot."

Liz followed her out to her car and they went to one of the nicer restaurants in town. Someone else better be paying for this lunch.

At the restaurant, Dr. Bennett greeted a tall man who looked to be in his forties. He was bald on top, with a fringe of hair worn unusually long, as if to provide an average amount of hair overall. He took Dr. Bennett's hands in both of his and leaned down to kiss her cheek. "Dora, my dear, you look fantastic! I swear, you never age."

Dr. Bennett bared her teeth at him. "Thank you for letting me know you're in town. I'm glad to have the opportunity to introduce you to Liz, and she's looking forward to hearing all about your research."

Yes, Dr. Bennett would only let him get away with comments on her appearance if she had an ulterior motive. Liz was surprised to hear Dr. Bennett called by her first name, too—she used Dr. DA Bennett, PhD, on publications to avoid having reviewers prejudge her work by her gender. Liz wondered if they were really challenging sexism when successful women hid their sex. But once again, Dr. Bennett was more interested in her own success than anyone else's struggle.

"I'm sure you won't find my little projects terribly exciting," Dr. Collins said. "You must be doing fascinating work yourself." He turned and studied Liz. "And this is the protégé? I've heard so many good things about you."

Liz offered her hand, but he grabbed her shoulders and kissed her cheek. She stiffened, too startled to do anything else.

"Let's be seated." Dr. Collins waved them into the restaurant with a bow, as if he were the maître d'. Once they'd passed him, he hurried around them to lead the way.

Since his back was to her, Liz scrubbed the damp spot on her cheek with her knuckles. Then she wanted to wash her hands.

He pulled out a chair for Dr. Bennet. "I daresay I've gotten us the best table, by the window and away from the flow of traffic. The menu looks quite good. You are fortunate to have such a quality restaurant in a town this size. Of course, I'm used to having a wide selection of good restaurants, but that's in a bigger city."

He talked non-stop as they looked at their menus. When the server came over, Dr. Collins asked, "Is the veal good? I'm sure it is. You wouldn't serve it if it wasn't. Veal for me, and for the young lady, I think." He smiled and nodded at Liz.

"Actually, I was planning to get the lasagna," she said.

"Oh, but really, I'm sure the veal is better," he said. "You need to know what to order in a place like this. It's not merely a matter of looking for the most expensive items, though that does provide a clue. You want something that must be cooked fresh, with the freshest ingredients. Lasagna can hide a variety of sins."

Liz gave the server a tight smile. "Lasagna, please." She didn't eat veal for ethical reasons. She would refrain from explaining that now, since she didn't want to embarrass Dr. Collins—or annoy Dr. Bennett—but she wasn't going to allow him to order it for her even if he was paying. And if he *wasn't* buying, at least she'd ordered one of the less expensive menu items, no matter how sinful her lasagna might be.

Dr. Collins kept up a stream of chatter while they waited for the food. He even managed to dominate the conversation while they were eating, as if he timed his bites to theirs to make sure no one else had a moment to speak. He praised the veal, then admitted that the lasagna looked and smelled very good, and then scolded Liz for not taking his lead in ordering the veal. The really astonishing thing was how he spoke so much and said so little. He praised everything without showing any real insight into it, and he did it in a way that flattered himself because he was expert enough to know what to praise.

Liz tried to imagine getting information out of him that was worth sharing with her soon-to-be-former advisor. She could barely imagine getting the basic information she'd need for her job if she was working for him.

She glanced at Dr. Bennett, surprised that the domineering woman she knew and feared would let this rather silly man control the conversation. But Dr. Bennett ate her food with no indication that she was even listening. She probably knew Dr. Collins well enough to realize he wouldn't give away anything valuable over lunch, which was why she wanted to get Liz into his lab.

Finally Liz couldn't stand it anymore. She got a bite of lasagna on her fork and lifted it toward her mouth, pausing an inch short of her lips. As soon as Dr. Collins had filled *his* mouth, she lowered her fork. "I'd love to hear more about your lab and the duties I might have if I'm lucky enough to get the postdoc position."

"Oh, there's so much to cover, we hardly have time to get started! And maybe it isn't an appropriate topic while eating."

"I'm certain whatever you have to share is absolutely fascinating." Great, half an hour together and she was starting to sound like him. "Dr. Bennett tells me you're doing some innovative research."

"I have recently gotten an enormous grant," Dr. Collins said. "That is what will allow me to take on an extra postdoc. It is really quite flattering to get the recognition." He went on about the grant and how grateful he was to receive the honor, saying nothing about his actual work.

By the time they finished eating, with tiny cups of coffee after, Liz had all she could take of the man. On the bright side, the lasagna had been tasty, she'd been famished, and Dr. Collins paid.

As he handed over a credit card, he said, "I'll put it on the expense report. They're very generous about approving expenses, at least for me. I know all the ladies in that department, and I daresay they know I won't abuse the system." Then he pulled out his phone. "I need to call Kevin—that's my current postdoc—and let him know to pick me up. It's so nice to have someone to drive, isn't it?"

Dr. Bennett shot a look at Liz. "I imagine it is."

Liz tried to keep her face bland and pleasant. She absolutely did not mention the number of times she'd driven Dr. Bennett somewhere, dropped her off, and then had to search for parking before scurrying to whatever meeting or event they were attending. At least she'd learned one more thing about Dr. Collins. He might pay for lunch to impress a potential future postdoc, but current postdocs didn't even get invited to the table. Unless Kevin had made some excuse to miss lunch because he thought no meal was worth spending more time with Dr. Collins, which was equally plausible.

Dr. Bennett said goodbye, tolerating another kiss on the cheek, and led Liz outside. "I know, he's tedious. It's hard to believe he's doing anything worthwhile, but he's gotten big grants." She gave an annoyed sniff.

Liz understood the frustration. This guy was at least two decades younger than Dr. Bennett was and apparently got more funding. Maybe he bored people until they gave him money to end the conversation, but more likely sexism played into it. So much for changing the world by using your initials. Or even by giving up your personal life and driving your students to the brink of madness.

She told Dr. Bennett, "I didn't get much sleep last night, because of the roof collapsing in the middle of the night. I think I'll walk home—well, where I'm staying until I find someplace more permanent—and ..." She couldn't bring herself to say *take a nap*. "Do some work there."

Dr. Bennett glared at her. "Don't think I don't know what you're doing. You keep hinting about something terrible happening last night, trying to get me to feel sorry for you. You'll never make it if you use every little inconvenience as an excuse to be lazy. I worked from my hospital bed after surgery and was back in the office the day they released me. That's how you get where I am."

Yeah, and by abusing your underlings and then asking them to spy on your opponents for you. I don't ever want to be you. The words almost came out. She really needed to take the rest of the day off or she'd say something she might regret later.

"I'll walk from here." Liz strode away.

Wait—she was heading toward her old apartment. She now had a lot farther to go than that. But if Liz went back to Dr. Bennett for a ride, she'd look foolish—and probably only get a ride back to the lab along with a longer lecture about her work ethic. Then she really would say something regrettable.

Well, if William had taken the day off to play chauffeur, she might as well make use of him.

She found his card and texted the number. She couldn't assume he was sitting around waiting for her call, so it might take him a while to get there. It was too cold to stand outside, she'd had lunch, and shopping was pointless when she had little money to buy things and no place to put them. She asked him to pick her up at the cat café. She might as well watch some cats, but first she'd go see what was happening at the apartment.

She stopped across the street from where she'd lived for almost three years. It had been a long time since she'd really looked at the building, a three-story brick structure that held a mixture of one-bedroom and two-bedroom apartments. A row of bushes filled the few feet between the building and the street, with a paved parking lot behind the building. The lack of a yard was one reason it had filled with twentysomethings and seniors rather than families with children.

The only real sign of the night's disaster was the yellow caution tape across the front door. Yet the building seemed oddly quiet and empty, as if abandoned for good. Maybe that was her imagination filling in the blanks of what she knew to be true.

According to the group chat initiated by Mrs. Aguilar, the landlord had informed the management company of the disaster, but with other houses and businesses suffering storm damage, no one knew when workers could get to theirs. The company was willing to refund the rest of the month's rent and their security deposits but wanted everyone to sign waivers in return, stating they wouldn't hold the company liable for any damages or losses. It would also end their current rental contracts. People speculated that the owner was hoping to use the insurance payout to do a complete renovation or even knock down the building and replace it with a newer one. If that happened, their low-rent apartments would be replaced by ones they couldn't afford.

Mrs. Aguilar and Mrs. Phan were threatening lawsuits unless everyone was allowed to return to their apartments once they reopened, at the same rent, without having to pay rent during the time the building was inaccessible. They were also pestering the management company to provide daily updates on repairs.

Liz admired the women for their fighting spirit and hoped they would succeed, but she personally didn't care about going back there. The apartment wasn't home; it was merely where she'd been living. Liz would have her PhD soon, and then ... Then what?

If things developed between Jade and Carl the way they seemed to be heading, Jade would marry Carl and have kids and rescue cats. Liz and Jade would stay friends, but they wouldn't be roommates forever.

She turned away from the apartment building and walked toward the cat café, deep in thought. Liz might turn into another Dr. Bennett. She shuddered at the idea. She desperately did not want to work for Dr. Collins, but what choice did she have? It wasn't like postdoc positions—or full-time research jobs—were easy to find. If she turned down Dr. Collins, it would annoy Dr. Bennett, and she'd have burned two bridges.

She stopped outside the café and looked through the windows. A man sat at a table, typing away at a laptop. The fluffy white cat on his lap tried to climb onto the keyboard, and he nudged it away. An older couple at another table sipped drinks and shared what looked like coffee cake. The man stroked a black and white cat with his free hand.

Liz shifted her gaze to a cat curled up in a hammock stuck to the glass with suction cups. It stretched and scratched its chin with its back paw.

She'd been working toward the PhD for so long. She'd put off other parts of her life—serious dating, pets, volunteer work, a social life beyond an occasional hour or two hanging out with Jade. The goal was the PhD. After that, things were supposed to be different. Better. But now she could only picture a future of working exhausting hours, chasing research grants, working just as hard for the next opportunity. Putting up with annoying men who would try to keep her fetching coffee and typing up reports instead of doing her own work. Working with women who wanted to see her suffer the way they had instead of supporting her career.

She hugged her computer bag to her chest, shivering in the damp breeze, and tried not to cry.

Chapter 9

Liz was vaguely aware of cars passing and one pulling into an empty space along the street. Lost in her thoughts, she didn't register the man who got out and approached her until he stopped a couple of feet away.

"Liz? Are you all right?" William lifted his hands as if ready to grab her should she collapse.

"Of course." She tossed her head, trying to shake away the thoughts, and loosened her grip on her bag, letting it hang over her shoulder again. "I'm fine. That was quick."

William studied her for a few seconds. Finally he said, "How was your lunch?"

Liz huffed out a short laugh. "The food was good. The company was there."

The corner of his mouth quirked up. "One of those, huh? I've suffered through meetings where the best thing was the catered sandwiches. You look cold. Let's get you in the warm car." He waved her toward it and opened the door for her.

She slid onto the leather seat, which cradled her like a warm hug. He must have turned on the seat warmer earlier. When the door closed, a shiver racked her body. She had herself under control by the time William got in the driver's side and started the car. She smiled at him. "Thank you for picking me up."

"Of course. Where to?"

"Carl's, I guess. I don't know what I'm doing today, but I need a break from the lab." From the world, really.

He pulled out from the parking spot. "I'm sorry your lunch wasn't more pleasant, but do you think it was useful?"

"I don't know. This guy apparently has a postdoc position I might get." Liz drew in a deep breath and sighed it out. "But I'm not sure I could tolerate him for an entire day, let alone a year. I almost wish I didn't have the opportunity."

"You can turn down opportunities if they're not right for you."

Liz scoffed. "Easy for you to say. What if it's the only opportunity I get?"

William frowned and didn't say anything. Ha! She'd won that round. Did he think it was easy to get into coveted positions? Maybe it was for him, with his family name and fortune. Liz was ordinary. Her parents both had PhDs and academic jobs, but they weren't in Liz's field. They probably couldn't help her, and she'd never ask, because she was sick of people acting like they were doing her a huge favor by helping her get something terrible. Why couldn't people succeed on their merits instead of connections?

She might as well ask why the Easter Bunny didn't leave baskets filled with wine and grant money instead of chocolate. No, in addition to chocolate. You had to have the chocolate too.

"I'm going to make a comparison," William said. "It's just a metaphor."

"Okay?"

"Would you marry someone because they asked you, and it's possible no one else will?"

"Of course not." Weird question, but the answer came easily.

Then Liz got what he was really saying. "Right. I concede the point, but ... I don't know."

Obviously she'd rather be on her own than with somebody she didn't love. Or maybe there was nothing obvious about it. She knew people determined to be married by thirty, so they could have children before forty. And plenty of people stayed in miserable relationships. But she could do without romantic love. She didn't want to do without it, but she could.

A job was different. Wasn't it?

"I'm in no mood to think about it," Liz grumbled. Once she actually got her PhD she could worry about the rest.

Liz imagined trying to work in Carl's house. Her room there didn't have a desk, and she'd never been comfortable working on her laptop while sitting on a bed.

She thought out loud. "If we're going to be at Carl's house very long, I'll need to set up a workstation. My room, I mean the guestroom I'm in, is lovely but doesn't have a desk."

Could she borrow the kitchen table? Carl and Jade would probably be gone until dinnertime, but what about Caroline?

"You can set up an office at my place," William said.

Liz studied him. That seemed to go beyond the call of whatever duty he might feel toward Carl. What was William's game? Finally she said, "Thanks, but it would be easier to have my workspace close to where I'm sleeping. It's bad enough that I can't walk to the lab from Carl's house."

"My house is behind Carl's. There's a fence between our backyards. You can walk between the houses in under two minutes."

"Oh." Liz couldn't think of an argument against that. William probably had plenty of extra room, so she could stay out of his way. Anyway, he'd usually be at work during the day. It sounded okay. "Thanks."

They were silent for a while. Liz studied William from the corner of her vision. He seemed to be frowning over his thoughts. Maybe he was regretting his offer.

"Did you get Sausage?" she asked to break the silence.

"Yes, he's fine. He's at my house so you can see him there."

"That's very generous of you. I'll get him out of there as soon as possible."

"It's fine. He has his own room."

Before she could pick apart that statement, he asked, "What would you do if you could do anything?"

"Ugh. That's a terrible question. It's like asking what I'd do if I had a million dollars. I don't have it and I'm not going to get it, so what's the point of deciding what I'd buy?" She scowled at him. "I suppose you do have a million dollars."

He shrugged, not denying it. "And I still don't know what I want to do with my life."

"What's that supposed to mean? You have a job. I'm guessing you have enough money you don't actually have to keep your job. That would suggest you like it."

"I don't dislike it. Some days I like it. I'm doing something, which is better than doing nothing."

"I guess so." She pondered for a minute. "Yeah, if I had all the money I needed to survive for the rest of my life, I wouldn't quit working. I'd get too bored. But I don't know if I'd keep a full-time job. I might start my own research lab if I had the funds for it, or do fieldwork. Not to study worms. Something with a higher level of intelligence." It was all solid scientific work, in theory, but she didn't get the thrill from working with worms that she might get from mammals.

"You're lucky to have that passion."

She was tempted to tease him about a lack of passion, but that seemed cruel when he was being vulnerable. "If you're not enthusiastic about your job, why do you keep it? You could travel the world, or ..." She waved vaguely. "I don't know, party with other rich people. Whatever it is rich people do. How is it you're so ordinary?" Liz winced. "I don't mean that in a bad way."

"No offense taken. I'd rather live an ordinary life." He blew out a breath. "Party with other rich people. Can you see me doing that?"

"You don't strike me as the partying type," she said carefully. "I'll admit most of my knowledge about rich families comes from the media. I pay as little attention as possible to the Kardashians or whatever rich kid is in the news for whatever excess. But it's impossible to entirely avoid hearing things, and, yeah, you don't fit the mold. How did that happen?"

"In my family, we don't just get a big trust fund at twenty-one. We can get money for school or traveling, and that's about it. I have a cousin who's an eternal student, studying a little bit of everything. She says she likes to learn things, although her grades don't support that claim. She does the minimum to keep her student status. Anyway, I didn't want to be a student at thirty—" He glanced at her. "Um, not that there's anything wrong with that."

"Hey, it wasn't exactly my dream either. I'm working as hard as I can to stop being a student."

They turned down a wide street with large trees and houses set well back from the street. Liz had never been in this part of town. William was driving, mostly not looking at her, and maybe that's what made him more talkative. She wanted to take advantage of the situation.

"But we were talking about you," she hinted.

One corner of his mouth twitched. "I work to feel useful, and so the businesses stay healthy and people like Carl can give away money. I wouldn't want his job—I don't have the people skills. I guess I don't really have big dreams. But if you do, you should follow them."

A weird shiver went through Liz. *Follow your dreams.* She'd heard that before, of course. It was a cliché or adage or something. But it hit her differently this time. Usually people assumed everyone had big dreams. They encouraged you to pursue those dreams—but in Liz's experience, only if your dreams were practical, achievable, and in line with what other people expected of you.

Her parents had nudged her away from the arts and toward science starting at a young age. They'd talked as if college, including advanced degrees, was a given. They wanted her to do well.

But Liz was lucky that her passion was in a field that got their approval. They wouldn't have supported her if her dreams had led her toward something like singing, acting, or fashion design. They definitely wouldn't have put her happiness first if she'd insisted she'd be happiest as a hairstylist or plumber. They might acknowledge that hairstylists and plumbers were useful and even needed, but those jobs were for other people. Not their child.

William turned in at a driveway that led to a white-painted house. Liz wasn't sure where she would have pictured William living, but this rambling old farmhouse wasn't it. She was glad for the distraction. She wasn't sure what else to say.

He pulled up to the house, turned off the car, and got out.

Liz scrambled out before he could get around the car to open her door. "This is your place?" Okay, dumb question, but she couldn't quite believe it

"Yes. I'll show you around and we can set up someplace for you to work."

She followed him onto the broad porch and waited while he unlocked the door. As he opened it, several dogs barked. Toenails clattered on the hardwood floor as they stepped inside and were surrounded by a blur of excited dogs.

"All these dogs are yours?" Liz asked.

"No, just that one." He pointed to the bulldog. "The Aguilars were overwhelmed with all the new animals, and I guess some of your neighbors are moving in with other family members or friends who can't take the pets. So I said I'd take the dogs for now, as well as Sausage. I'm not sure how well he'd get along with the dogs, so he's in a guest bedroom. You can take him back to Carl's if you want, or keep him here."

As the jumping and wriggling slowed down, Liz recognized the extra dogs. She crouched and gave out rubs and scratches in return for damp kisses. The bulldog seemed sweet, his whole back end wagging and his tongue hanging out as he jockeyed for position in the cuddle line. She had not imagined William with a bulldog, although it seemed to suit him perfectly.

Why had she expected something else?

Oh, right—at the café, George had said William had a vicious dog. It was hard to imagine the bulldog being vicious. But George and William had known each other as children, so possibly the dog that bit George was long gone. It seemed like George had implied William still had that dog, but maybe Liz had assumed that incorrectly.

Was it only yesterday that she had met George? Now she struggled to remember what he had said. George had warned her against William, and at the time she'd thought the warning unnecessary, since she planned to see as little of him as possible. And now look at them! Once again it seemed life didn't care about her plans.

In any case, maybe William had learned his lesson about dangerous dogs. Now he was a grownup with responsibilities. He was awkward and ... grumpy wasn't quite the right word. But even when he was doing so much to help Liz and taking in strangers' pets, he seemed distant, almost indifferent. But he wasn't mean.

Liz pushed to her feet, feeling better for the dog slobber on her cheek and multicolored fur clinging to her jeans.

"Okay, dogs, out back again." William led them through the house to the back door and shooed them out. The door had a dog flap, which explained how all the animals had been in the house when they arrived.

"I put Sausage in here." He opened a door.

Liz stepped into a small, cheerful room with white walls and a window providing light. A single bed had a quilt on it that looked handmade. Sausage had claimed a spot in the middle of the quilt. Liz glanced at William to see how he would take this.

He closed the door behind them. A wave of ... something washed over Liz, leaving her short of breath.

But it was fine. No need to feel like she was in danger. He'd closed the door to keep Sausage in, of course. And now he was standing in front of it—not blocking it; he'd merely stopped once he'd entered the room—looking just as detached as always.

Liz stepped away from him. She sat on the edge of the bed, letting her bag slide off her shoulder. She petted Sausage and told her nervous system to stop overreacting. She'd had too many shocks lately. No wonder she was waiting for the next disaster.

"Hey, baby," she cooed as she rubbed Sausage's cheek. Then her brain caught up to her words. Warmth flooded her face, but she refused to glance at William to see if he'd reacted. She wasn't sure what would be worse—interest, amusement, or scorn.

After a few seconds, William said, "You can work in this room if you'd like. The litter box is in here." He crossed to the open closet door and crouched. A scuffing sound suggested he was scooping litter or at least stirring it to cover up messes. The cat hater was not only taking in her cat but scooping its litter? It boggled the mind.

But William probably wanted to get rid of the smell, or the reminder of a cat in his house, or something. He seemed kind of uptight and finicky. No doubt he'd sterilize the room once Sausage was gone. Although he couldn't be too uptight about keeping his lovely house pristine if he had a dog and allowed strangers' dogs to run around it unsupervised.

Liz didn't know what to think, so she decided to stop thinking about it.

He stood and turned to look at her expectantly. Wait, what had he said?

"Or I can show you some other rooms," he said. "I thought you might like to be in here with Sausage, but I have plenty of space ... You can use my office this afternoon, but there might be times I need it. We can make changes in here if you want." He frowned at the sturdy wooden desk that sat in the corner opposite the bed.

Right, she could use the room. The chair pushed under

the desk didn't quite fit the room's old-fashioned, cozy vibe, being a padded office chair on rollers, but it would certainly be more comfortable than a wooden chair. Sausage seemed to have survived his ordeal in good spirits, but it might comfort him to have a familiar face around.

Okay, it would comfort her to have Sausage's familiar face around.

"This room will be fine. Better than fine, actually. It's very nice. Practically perfect." Great, now she was rambling. She stood and faced him. "Thank you for all your kindness."

He shook his head. "No thanks necessary. I'm just glad you're all right."

All right. Was she? She swallowed. "Yeah, the last twenty-four hours—twelve hours?" It felt like days. Could it really be right that she'd been awoken by a crash at three a.m. that morning? "Whatever. They've been rough."

It all came crashing back on her—being startled awake, the panicked evacuation, trying to get everyone and a few important things out quickly, in case more ceilings collapsed, not knowing where they'd sleep that night. The exhaustion, the enormous list of things to be done, her despair at the thought of working for Dr. Collins, her frustration and anger at Dr. Bennett.

Tremors shook her body. Her breath came quickly. She couldn't get enough air.

"Hey!" He took two steps toward her, lifted his hands, and hesitated. She stared at him helplessly. Finally he dropped his hands to her shoulders, squeezing gently. "It's—you're—whatever it is, we'll deal with it."

Liz couldn't help herself. She stepped forward, slowly so he could back away if he wanted to. He didn't, so she dropped her forehead to his shoulder. He was the last person she'd choose for this but the only one available, and she really needed a hug.

For a moment, their only points of contact were his

hands on her shoulders and her forehead against his shoulder. Then his arms came around her, tucking her close. "Shh," he murmured. "I've got you. It will be all right."

His arms were firm around her, his body warm enough to soothe the chill. With her cheek pressed to his chest, his heartbeat sounded faintly in her ear, strong and steady.

She could almost believe him.

Chapter 10

William went to his own home office and tried to get some work done. It was weird knowing Liz was right down the hall. That *shouldn't* interfere with his work, since he couldn't see or hear her. Yet he couldn't concentrate. Too many changes lately, maybe. He had a cat in his house, and extra dogs, and Liz—but thinking about all that wasn't going to help his focus.

He had dozens of emails to answer, and some of the family message threads had blown up due to the storm. He suspected that in most families, message threads contained more small talk and personal updates. In his family, that quickly gave way to business and charity topics. Also occasionally arguments, accusations, defenses, and whining. That probably was like most families. William tried to stay out of it. He just wanted to keep things running smoothly and avoid drama.

He caught up on the conversations and sighed. He added to the thread: *I'll talk to Carl.*

Technically William didn't have a role in the charitable foundation, but he had recommended Carl for the job. It was more a favor to the foundation than to Carl, since Carl was sensible and dependable, which the position needed, and also cheerful and generous enough to enjoy working with the groups that got donations. The downside was that now people often expected William to pass along messages. Why couldn't they just contact Carl directly? People insisted it was easier this way. Easier for them, maybe.

William messaged Carl and then started wading through his other work while trying to ignore the fact that he had an interesting woman in a room down the hall. Out of sight was not out of mind in this case.

When Carl's response came, William closed his files. The guestroom door was shut, so Liz must still be ensconced there. Or else she'd slipped out already, but

William had left his office door open and hadn't heard anything. Surely she'd be polite enough to say goodbye. She was snarky but not rude.

William had hoped to escort her over to Carl's for dinner, but he didn't want to interrupt if she was working or napping. If she came out and wondered where he was, she could call or message him—or find her way on her own, since he'd already explained that Carl's house was across the backyard. It wasn't exactly a challenging or dangerous commute. He had no excuse to disturb her.

The dogs greeted William noisily as he left the house. He spent a few minutes petting them, partly for the enjoyment and partly to make sure the dogs felt welcome, and maybe a little so if Liz had been alerted by the racket, she could find him. But she did not appear.

Finally he strode across the backyard, a hundred-foot stretch of native grasses with a path beaten through the middle. The dogs crowded around him. He often brought Rufus to Carl's, but he probably shouldn't show up with a whole pack. He stepped over the low gate.

The lab-retriever mix leapt over after him. The gate was tall enough to block his bulldog, the Chihuahua, and the elderly poodle that appeared to have hip problems. The mystery mutt whined and jumped against the gate. It looked like he might get over if he tried for long enough and got lucky.

Right. Okay. If William was going to have these dogs here, he'd have to check the whole perimeter to make sure none of them could escape. The Chihuahua might be small enough to slip through a gap Rufus couldn't, and clearly the fence wouldn't keep the lab in. So far they must have enjoyed playing with the pack more than escaping, but how long would that last?

William rubbed his temples. He normally lived a quiet life. He *liked* a quiet life. He didn't want all this upheaval in his routines. But he had a level of privilege most people didn't, so he had a responsibility to help when he could.

Besides, if he was entirely honest with himself, he'd enjoyed this day more than he would've expected. Meeting Mrs. Aguilar, clearly a force to be reckoned with. Getting to know the extra dogs. Spending time with Liz. Helping ease some of her stress. She seemed more annoyed at needing help than grateful for it, which he understood. Loud thanks would only make him uncomfortable anyway. But he thought she'd appreciated the rides and the workspace. She had too much else to deal with. Maybe he couldn't solve all her problems—and he doubted she'd take the attempt kindly—but he could give her a bit of peace and quiet.

He'd definitely had worse days.

He didn't have a ball on him, but he found a stick, got the lab's attention with it, and flung it hard into his own yard. The dog leapt back over the gate and took off after it, all the others tagging along. William hurried to Carl's house. If he was lucky, the dogs would get distracted and forget about him. Out of sight, out of mind might work on animals with a shorter attention span. He'd come back in a few minutes to feed them and then keep them inside for the night so they couldn't stray.

William called out as he entered Carl's back door and heard a yelled response from the kitchen. He found Carl chopping vegetables and Caroline sitting at the kitchen table painting her nails. William had hoped to speak to Carl alone, but at least Jade wasn't there. She might be somewhere else in the house though. "Where's Jade?" he asked.

"She'll be at work for another hour," Carl said. "Fortunately, it doesn't sound like the storm did permanent damage to the cat rescue, since they had backup generators, but I guess there's still a lot to clean and fix. She works so hard! I really admire her dedication."

Caroline held up her hand and studied the alternating pink and purple nails. "Jade seems nice. Not like her friend, what's-her-name. She's uptight and kind of mean."

"No she's not, if you're talking about Liz," William said. "Look, Carl, can I talk with you privately for a minute?"

"Caroline, will you keep an eye on the sauce?" Carl waved toward a pot bubbling on the stove.

She wiggled her fingers. "I can't touch anything until they dry. Come on, William, you don't have any secrets from me, do you?" She smiled flirtatiously.

He hesitated. He didn't like talking business in front of Caroline, but she'd find out soon enough. In fact, if he made a fuss about privacy, she'd probably listen at the door or badger Carl for information later, and then she'd make a bigger deal out of it.

"Okay. It's just business stuff anyway, nothing exciting." He leaned on the counter next to his friend. "Carl, have you written the checks for this month's donations?"

"Not yet. I've been finalizing the paperwork. I was going to write checks tomorrow. Why?"

"The food pantry got hit by lightning last night. They lost power, and their backup generator exploded."

"Exploded!"

"No one was hurt, but they have a lot of fused wires, a useless generator, and at least one of the commercial refrigerators can't be saved. They lost several thousand dollars' worth of refrigerated and frozen food. They really need ten thousand dollars right away in order to keep up services. Demand is going to be high, since some of their clients lost power as well. They'll need to replace spoiled foods and might have additional repair expenses due to the storm."

"That's terrible. Of course we'll help." Carl chopped some more vegetables. William waited for the implication to sink in. "Oh. You want me to pay them from next month's charitable allocation. That's everything that's not already assigned each month."

"Yes."

"I promised ... But this is urgent. We can't let people go hungry."

"Right. We can probably do some additional fundraising or adjust the donation amounts next month, but that will take time, and meetings with the accountants and lawyers, and probably a vote."

"Yeah." Carl's shoulders sagged. "Jade will understand, I'm sure."

Caroline pushed back her chair. "Obviously people are more important than cats."

"That might depend on who you ask," Carl said with a wry grin.

"You're so sweet, Willie, trying to take care of everyone." Caroline moved toward William, holding her hands with her fingers spread. They reminded him of bloody claws.

He backed around the kitchen island. He didn't trust her concern for her fingers enough to assume she wouldn't try to make contact. "Well, I should get back and see how Liz is doing. She's using one of my spare rooms as an office."

Caroline pouted. "Why does she need a room in your house? She already has a room here."

"She needed a desk. Anyway, I picked up their cat today and he's at my house."

"You're too generous," Caroline muttered.

Carl chuckled. "Caro, you just complimented him on being sweet for taking care of people."

"That's different. Those food pantry people need help. They're, like, homeless and stuff."

"Some are but many aren't," Carl said. "They just need some extra help."

"You do realize Liz and Jade are literally without a home, right?" William asked.

"I guess, but why don't they move in with family or other friends. You just met them!"

Carl turned from the counter and gave his sister a stern look. "I don't know enough of their family situation to answer that, but not everybody can count on family or friends in times like this."

"You're saying they *don't* have friends?" Caroline smirked. "That must say something about them."

"I'm sure they have friends," Carl said. "But we don't know whether the friends have extra room or are in difficult situations themselves. We have the space, so we can share it."

"Maybe *you're* too generous," Caroline grumbled. "I'm sure William is more sensible about these things." She flashed him a smile.

He shrugged. "Liz is in my house right now, along with a cat I'm allergic to and five dogs that aren't mine. Speaking of which, I should go feed them."

"Grab Liz and come back for dinner," Carl said. "I'm making pasta arrabbiata."

He must really like Jade if he was cooking a dish he usually saved for special occasions. "Okay. See you soon." William escaped. At least he'd delivered his unfortunate message and avoided Caroline's hugs.

The dogs escorted William back to his house. He ushered them inside, shushing them as they passed the guest room. In the kitchen, he consulted a list. His bulldog and the poodle had special senior diets, so he took them into the laundry room. The bulldog sat heavily, looked at the low-calorie food, and gave a world-weary sigh.

"Sorry, Rufus, you know the vet said you need to lose some weight for your health. You have enough trouble breathing with that short nose. You don't need heart problems too."

Back in the kitchen, he scooped up the Chihuahua. "And you need a diet for sensitive stomachs, apparently. You'll have to eat outside while I keep the other dogs in." He latched the pet door shut and put the Chihuahua and her food on the back porch. He squeezed back in, trying to block the opening with his body to keep the other dogs from escaping. "Now knock it off. You can't have that food. Yes, I realize variety might be nice. I promise, those guys don't have anything better then you're going to get."

The mystery mutt yipped.

"Your friends will be back in no time. I ..." He trailed off as he saw Liz leaning against the kitchen archway. How much had she heard? "Hi."

"Need any help?" She looked amused.

"No." He started filling the other dog dishes and remembered to add, "Thanks. How was your afternoon?"

"Better than my morning." She yawned. "I got caught up on email and talked to Mrs. Aguilar. Then Sausage and I took a nap on that bed."

"Good." He couldn't think of anything to say for a minute. "Carl is cooking. He says we should come over for dinner."

"Oh. That's nice of him, but I don't know if I can handle more people today. I'm not in a social mood."

"Totally understandable. You can stay here if you want. Or get some of Carl's pasta and go to your room over there. Carl will understand."

Liz raised an eyebrow. "Will Caroline?"

William hesitated. "Well, it won't bother her if you bow out."

Liz gave a short laugh. "She'll probably be glad to have me out of the way."

William was a terrible liar, so he usually didn't even try it. Instead he avoided awkward conversations if he could. But he had to give some kind of answer. "I know she's ... a lot, sometimes, but she's young, and she likes having her brother to herself."

Liz scoffed. "Yeah, it's her brother she wants to herself."

He didn't know how to answer that. He washed his hands and turned toward Liz. She leaned against the doorway, arms wrapped around herself as if she was cold.

"Should I turn up the heat?" he asked.

She shook her head. "I'll head over to Carl's. I'm pretty sure I packed some sweaters."

"Do you want a jacket for the walk?"

"It's, what, two minutes? I'll survive."

"We can do better than *survival*."

"Sometimes I wonder. It's fine." Her smile looked forced. He didn't like the idea that Liz felt the need to force anything around him. Pestering her about it wouldn't improve the situation though.

"Okay." The dogs had already finished eating. William let the ones with special diets back into the kitchen. He'd have to make sure he wasn't gone too long, so he could let out anyone who needed to go to the bathroom.

"What did you decide about Sausage?" he asked. "It's fine if he stays here. Just wondering."

She hesitated. "If you really don't mind, I'll leave him here for now. He's been through a lot of changes lately and he seems comfortable enough in that room."

"You don't think he's bothered by all the dogs?"

Her grin looked more natural. "I'm pretty sure he was trying to get their attention under the door so he could tease them for not being able to get at him."

William smiled back. "That's all right then. Let's go."

Chapter 11

At Carl's, Liz slipped into her room for a while but came out when she heard Jade enter the house. Carl greeted Liz warmly. "Have you explored the drink options in the fridge?" He dropped his voice to a whisper. "I wish I could offer you a beer, but I don't keep alcohol here, since Caroline is only twenty. I sometimes bring home a bottle of wine for a special occasion, but I don't keep it in the house."

"It's quite all right," Liz said. "Alcohol would put me to sleep and I don't need the help right now."

Somehow Liz got caught up in the conversation and ended up having dinner with the others after all. She needed food, and she wanted to exchange news with Jade anyway. Carl looked worried as Jade recounted the work they'd done at the rescue that day, but it seemed they had gotten everything under control after the storm—although the roof needed repairs, ideally before the next big rain.

Then Liz told everyone about her lunch meeting, imitating Dr. Collins in his effusive praise of everything. That helped her feel like she could laugh at the whole situation too.

"But what are you going to do?" Caroline asked. "Surely you can't turn down the job offer. What if you never get another?"

Liz was surprised that Caroline would echo her own worries, or that she cared in the least. She studied Caroline suspiciously, but the girl seemed innocent enough with her wide-eyed expression. And then she added, "You're already *homeless*. How will you ever get back on your feet if you don't take this job?"

Carl winced. William closed his eyes, and Liz thought she heard a faint groan.

"I've worked hard for this PhD," Liz said. "I will wait for the right opportunity. I don't need to be someone's servant to advance my career." She hesitated and then added, "Or if I do, it won't be his. I know what it's like to work with difficult people. Maybe I won't find a postdoc with anyone better than Dr. Collins, but I certainly can't find anyone worse!"

It felt good to say that out loud. She could do better. She would.

"Anyway, I have work with Dr. Bennett until the end of summer," she added, in case Carl or William started to suspect Liz planned to mooch off of them.

"You have plenty of time to find something better," Carl said.

Caroline frowned and opened her mouth, but Carl quickly changed the topic. "William, how are the new dogs getting along? And how are you getting along with them?"

"They're fine. It probably helps that dogs are generally pack animals, and I guess all the ones from Liz and Jade's building already knew each other."

"Poor Rufus!" Caroline cooed. "He's probably anxious for the strangers to get out of his house so he has you to himself."

"Rufus is having the time of his life," William said dryly. "It's like going to the dog park all day long. I may have to get him a pet of his own so he won't be lonely once the other dogs are back with their people."

Liz hadn't missed the unsubtle dig at houseguests, but Caroline was a guest too. Well, she was family and no doubt thought she had all kinds of extra privileges, including the right to be rude to Carl's other guests. But Carl was her brother, not her parent. Liz was an only child, but she didn't think brothers generally felt obligated to take in their sisters who were old enough to live on their own and take care of themselves.

In any case, it wasn't her problem. Liz kept her head down and focused on the meal. She enjoyed the pasta, which was spicy enough to leave her lips tingling. A couple more days of decent sleep and good meals, and she might recover from the storm and its repercussions.

Once everyone finished eating, Carl and William collected the dishes and carried them to the sink. Jade jumped up. "I'll do the dishes."

William whispered something to Carl, who turned to smile at Jade. At least his mouth looked like it was trying to smile. His expression gave Liz an anxious feeling.

"Actually, could I talk to you privately for a minute?" Carl asked Jade.

"Oh. Of course."

William started filling the dishwasher. Caroline jumped up. "I'll help William." She stood close beside him.

"You can put away the rest of that sauce, please," he said.

Liz decided not to offer her help. Too many cooks spoil the broth, and too many dishwashers break dishes. She followed Jade and Carl to the hallway.

"When you're done, come to my room," she told Jade. "We should go over the updates from Mrs. Aguilar and discuss next steps."

Especially if Carl's discomfort was because he was planning to ask them when they might be able to leave his hospitality. Dinner had been surprisingly pleasant, but something in the air made Liz feel off balance again.

"We won't be long." Carl guided Jade into his home office with a hand to her back.

"Oh no!" Caroline squealed. "I splattered myself with the pasta sauce."

Liz glanced back into the kitchen.

Caroline brushed at her shirt, pulling it down to reveal more cleavage. "William, do you think it will come out in the wash?"

"I don't know. Better go soak it right away." William closed the dishwasher and turned to look at Liz. "I'll head home."

"Oh, don't." Caroline pouted. "We could play a game or watch a movie. Wouldn't it be nice to cuddle up on the couch and watch something? Just let me clean up." She dipped a hand towel under running water and patted her chest, soaking her thin shirt.

"No thanks. I need to let out the dogs and do my own chores." William didn't look at Caroline. His somber gaze was on Liz. William had probably whispered to Carl that he ought to evict Liz and Jade, and now he was wondering if Carl was really tough enough to do it. Although William had practically invited her to stay at his house ...

"Thanks for everything today," she told William, because whatever else happened, he had made her life easier. "I'm going to my room."

Caroline glared at her. Should Liz not have referred to it as *her* room? Obviously it wasn't hers, but it was hers for the moment. She would have used the same term if staying in a hotel.

Liz glanced at William to see if he seemed equally offended. His gaze lingered on Liz as he rubbed his lips together. He must have found the pasta spicy enough to leave a tingle as well. Nice to know they were well matched in their heat tolerance.

No it wasn't! It didn't make the least bit of difference.

Finally he said, "Good night to you both."

Caroline scowled as he left without a backward glance. No doubt she would have chased after him if she hadn't been dripping wet and made a fuss about needing to clean her shirt.

Liz retreated to her room. She would keep thinking of it that way until Carl kicked them out. She was too tired to do anything productive, so she flopped on the bed and stared at the ceiling, waiting for Jade.

A few minutes later, Jade came in and closed the door behind her. She leaned against it, her head down and lower lip trembling.

Liz sat up and swung her legs around so she was sitting on the edge of the bed. "Is everything all right?"

"Yes. No." Jade sat next to Liz. "Carl says I can't have the money for the special needs rescue yet."

"What do you mean?" That came out loud. Liz dropped her voice. "I thought he'd basically promised it to you!"

"Yes, but I'm not the only one who needs funds. It's okay. I understand. I'm just disappointed." Jade managed a weak smile. "Is there anything we absolutely need to discuss tonight? It's been a long day. For both of us."

Liz ran over her list of discussion topics in her mind. "Everything can wait until tomorrow." Especially if they weren't being evicted.

"Good. I'm going to bed." Jade dragged herself upright and trudged the few steps to the door.

"Did he say anything about us being here?" Liz asked. "How long we have?"

Jade paused with her hand on the door handle. "Oh, that's fine. He said he's happy to have us for as long as we need a place to stay."

"Do you believe him?"

Jade's eyebrows went up. "Of course! Everyone has been so kind. You've seen how wrong you were about William and Caroline. William has been very pleasant, hasn't he?"

"Hm. I refuse to admit I was wrong." She lifted her chin and gave a sniff. "It's a terrible thing to be expected to be rational about people you've decided to hate."

Jade's look was affectionate. "People who didn't know you so well might not realize you're joking." She went out and closed the door behind her.

Was she joking? Liz wasn't sure. William had been quite agreeable that day. Very helpful, in fact.

As for Caroline, as William had said, she was young enough that it almost excused her jealousy and foolishness. If Liz was in a generous mood, which she rarely was, she could see how Caroline might become infatuated with her brother's tall, dark, and handsome friend. To his credit, William didn't seem to be encouraging it or taking the very broad hints.

A knock came at the door. Liz jumped. Had William

come back for something just as she was thinking about him? She cleared her throat and ignored the bizarre urge to fluff her hair. "Come in."

The door open to reveal Caroline. That was the last person Liz had expected. Not that she'd been looking forward to seeing William again. The odd feeling of disappointment wasn't because it wasn't him. It was only that Caroline had taken almost no interest in Liz at any point in their acquaintance.

"Can I help you?" Liz asked.

"Isn't that my line?" Caroline leaned against the wall. She'd changed into a dark T-shirt, so she'd decided no one remaining in the house needed to see her cleavage. "After all, you're a guest in my house and have made yourself quite comfortable."

"It is a comfortable room." Liz tried to keep her tone light. "But I was under the impression it's Carl's house."

"He's my brother, and I live here, so ..." She shrugged in a way that was oddly reminiscent of William. "Anyway, your kitten rescue or whatever isn't getting the money. I imagine you'll want to move out now."

"Do you?" Liz didn't want to let the bratty girl get to her, but it was hard to keep her expression bland.

Caroline opened her eyes wide. "Why would you want to stay here if Carl isn't giving you the money?"

"I don't see what the two things have to do with each other. We didn't stay here in order to get the money."

Another shrug. "If you say so, but you can't want to see Carl and William anymore."

"You shouldn't make assumptions." Liz forced herself to smile. "William has been very kind to me." She couldn't help adding, "Maybe I'll move in there if I'm not welcome here."

"No!" Caroline jerked up straight and then visibly forced herself to sink back into a relaxed pose. At least Liz was getting to her too. "Anyway, William is the one who told Carl not to give Jade the money."

Buzzing filled Liz's head. She felt hot and itchy and wanted to hit something. She swallowed and managed to say calmly enough, "Was he?"

Caroline nodded smugly. "Usually they let Carl decide, but this time William told him no. He must really not want your friend to help those poor little kittens. They're the ones with special needs, right? I guess they'll have to be put to sleep."

Liz stood and loomed over Caroline. "Get out."

Caroline shrank back, and this time the wide eyes didn't look like an attempt to be cute. After a moment she managed, "It's my house."

"Right now, this is my room. You have five seconds to get out of it, or I'll make you regret being here."

Caroline stomped out of the room with her chin high. Liz closed the door behind her. She leaned against it and waited for the hot rage to subside.

She'd probably gone too far. Caroline would complain to Carl, and maybe they really would get evicted. Not that she wanted to stay here any longer. Liz didn't want to have anything to do with any of them. But Jade was always more forgiving, and they didn't have a lot of options at the moment.

Liz rubbed her face. She ought to apologize. She couldn't, not yet. Caroline had crossed the line from youthful foolishness to cruelty. And William ...

Liz didn't want to think about him.

She needed to get some sleep so she could face all her problems in the morning. There had to be a way out that didn't involve asking Carl or William for anything.

Chapter 12

Liz was too angry to sleep well. Angry at William for sabotaging Jade's chance at a special needs cat rescue. Angry at Carl for not fighting William. Angry at Jade for being sad and understanding instead of furious.

Liz needed to get her life together—away from William, Carl, and Caroline. Then she could go back to merely being frustrated and annoyed with her dissertation advisor.

Her mood was not improved by reading an email from Dr. Collins first thing in the morning. He started with a rambling recitation of the lunch they'd shared. She'd been there; she knew how it had gone! Finally he got around to an invitation, or perhaps a summons, to meet with him that day.

Privately, without Dr. Bennett. That part suited Liz fine, as she didn't want Dr. Bennett to hear her turn down the postdoc position with Dr. Collins. Dr. Bennett had said Liz could defend her PhD by the end of summer. Liz might just escape if Dr. Bennett believed that Liz would be more useful to her out of the lab than in it.

On the other hand, Liz didn't want to be anywhere private with Dr. Collins. She didn't even want to share a meal with him. It should take less than five minutes to turn down a job, should one be offered, and she didn't want to waste a moment more than necessary. If only he'd made the job offer in the email, or asked for an application, or even told her she wasn't suitable! Then they could be done with this already.

But he hadn't, and it would be abrasive even by Liz's standards to refuse a job she hadn't yet gotten. She invited him to meet her at the cat café that morning. There she wouldn't be trapped for the length of a restaurant meal, but she could get coffee and a pastry for breakfast, because she was not going to rummage through Carl's kitchen and risk running into someone she didn't want to see. As a bonus, she could pet the cats to calm down and remember that while people often stank, they weren't the only animals in the world.

She showered, resenting how great that shower was, and put on casual clothes inappropriate for a job interview. On the way out, she thought she heard Carl and Jade speaking in low voices in the kitchen. Liz didn't want to hear anything they had to say, and she really didn't think they'd want to hear what she had to say. She snuck past the archway and slipped out of the house.

She got to the café fifteen minutes early and ordered. If she finished eating before Dr. Collins arrived, she could make a quicker escape. The extra time might also allow her to shake off her rotten mood. What better way to do that than with good coffee, an excellent piece of coffee cake, and lots of cats?

Liz made the rounds, petting several different cats, before finally settling down at a table near a calico identified as Charlotte by her photo on the wall. Charlotte was described as "a shy, sweet girl who rewards those who take the time to get to know her." Shy and sweet normally would not be Liz's kind of thing, but she needed some sweetness to balance her sour mood.

Charlotte sat on the bench in a tidy loaf and eyed Liz suspiciously while Liz focused on her breakfast. After a few minutes, the cat stretched, stood, and crept closer. Without making eye contact, Liz held her hand to the side until Charlotte decided to sniff it and finally rubbed her cheek against Liz's knuckles. Five minutes after that, Charlotte was in Liz's lap.

By the time Liz had a belly full of coffee cake and caffeine firing up her brain, she'd relaxed enough to be only slightly irritated that Dr. Collins was late. She'd give him five more minutes. If he didn't show, then she'd have an excuse to leave without talking to him!

Moments after she had the thought, she spotted his tall form coming down the hallway. He frowned at the barista counter, looked through the window at Liz, and waved. He opened the cat room door without stopping to order anything.

The barista called out to him. With the door open, Liz heard Dr. Collins say, "But I'm not staying. I'll only be a few minutes talking to the young lady in here."

Oh, right, if you didn't order at least ten dollars' worth of food or drink, you had to pay to hang out with the cats. Most people used that as an excuse to buy some of the delicious baked goods.

Well, if Liz and Dr. Collins had to talk in the hallway, it would be that much faster. She started to shift the cat off her lap so she could stand.

Charlotte dug her claws into Liz's thigh. Liz yelped and sank back down. Charlotte never even stopped purring.

"I really don't see the point of paying to hang out with animals," Dr. Collins was saying, "and ordinary animals too, not something exotic like at a zoo." He had his back to Liz but must have passed over some money, because he turned with an annoyed look and pushed through the door.

"I honestly don't see what all the fuss is about. Good morning, Miss Boyd. I'm glad you could meet me today. I'm looking forward to furthering our acquaintance." He sat facing her. "I am not particularly a cat person, but that is a pretty creature. I must confess, I don't understand why people would pay money to come here and visit with cats they don't own. It seems strange, doesn't it?"

"Not at all." Liz was delighted to start disagreeing with him right away. "Not everyone can keep cats in their homes. They may live in an apartment that forbids pets. Someone might have a roommate who's allergic. They might travel a lot. The café gives people a chance to spend time with cats in a safe, casual setting, with the bonus of good food and drink. And all of these cats are adoptable, so I believe people also come here when they're interested in getting a cat. They can test drive one, so to speak."

"Well, it still seems odd to me, but I will defer to your greater experience in this matter. I trust I have areas of expertise, but I am not so conceited that I can't admit an occasional deficiency in my knowledge. Now, shall we get down to business?" Dr. Collins then proceeded to talk for ten minutes straight about his lab and what he required in an assistant, without actually getting down to any relevant business—such as asking Liz to do something so she could refuse.

Finally she interrupted. "Dr. Collins, I appreciate you taking time out of your busy schedule to speak to me. But we both have a lot to do, so ..." *Get on with it*, she thought. *Don't make me ask if you're going to offer me the job when I'm going to say no.*

"Very good!" he said. "Practical and to the point. I like that. I need someone to keep me on track. Once in a while I tend to get distracted or wander off topic." He chuckled. "It has been suggested to me that I ought to have a wife. Someone to listen to me talk at home, so maybe I wouldn't feel so obliged to share all my thoughts with my students and colleagues. I'm not saying I would turn down the opportunity ..." He studied Liz in a considering way she did not like. "But finding a wife isn't as easy as that."

"No, I imagine it isn't." Liz managed a tight smile. "But I'm afraid I'm not available for the postdoc position, or any position in your lab."

"What?" He frowned. "I must say, most young people show more gratitude for opportunities such as this. You may have had success on the dating scene playing hard to get, but it is most inappropriate when being offered a job opportunity, especially such a fine position as this one."

"I'm not playing hard to get. I don't want the job."

"But Dr. Bennett indicated ..."

"Dr. Bennett doesn't know my plans. In fact, if I can ask a very great favor of you, I would appreciate it if you don't tell her about this."

Letting him know she didn't want Dr. Bennett to find

out was a risk, but Liz suspected Dr. Bennett would avoid Dr. Collins, and if they did see each other, Dr. Collins wouldn't get to the point. Any point.

She added, "I'm anxious to finish my PhD, and she suggested a willingness to move along the process if I had a job waiting."

"Well, then, I don't see why you wouldn't be interested in working under me. I assure you it would be a very comfortable position."

She narrowed her gaze. Had that been suggestive, or was he really that clueless? She honestly couldn't tell, so she let it go. "I'm sure, but I have other plans. I prefer to keep them private for now."

"I see." He frowned for a few moments. "I suppose I can understand the desire for privacy. Some people are such gossips, aren't they?" He sighed. "Well, I suppose I will have to be disappointed. I really was looking forward to having a bright, pretty young lady in the lab."

Liz was momentarily speechless. Or rather, she had so many things to say that she couldn't get any of them out. *Pretty.* As if that was relevant in the workplace. Should she point out the inappropriateness of that comment?

But he wasn't her problem, and she wanted him to do her the favor of keeping quiet. It went against every instinct, but she bit back the reply she would have liked to make. Her hand must have tightened on Charlotte though, because the cat flexed her claws, not actually breaking skin but letting Liz know they were there.

That gave Liz an idea. "You know, it may be difficult to get a wife, but it isn't difficult to get a companion. Perhaps a pretty little lady like this one?" She gently turned Charlotte toward Dr. Collins. Charlotte gave a cute little *meep.*

"I am not really a cat person." But he studied Charlotte with some interest.

"Have you ever had a cat before?" Liz asked.

"No. I've never had pets. My parents did not approve

of keeping animals in the home."

"Then how do you know you couldn't become a cat person? They're ideal pets for busy people, since they don't have to be walked like dogs. She'll greet you when you come home each night, providing affection and listening to you talk about your day as much as you like. All she'll ask in return is affection, food, and water." She added lightly, "and of course a litter box and vet care."

He really couldn't ask for anyone better to listen to him ramble. Granted, cats were known to show their indifference, but Liz doubted Dr. Collins would notice if Charlotte turned her back on him or groomed herself while he talked. Shy Charlotte would do well as an only cat with a lonely bachelor, not like Lydia who demanded so much attention.

"Perhaps." He reached slowly toward Charlotte. She lifted a paw and batted gently at his fingers.

"Here, sit back and I'll slide her onto your lap." The cat might get flustered and take off, but Liz did not want to hold the cat on her lap while Dr. Collins had his hands on Charlotte. Liz had come very close to getting through this encounter without offending him or becoming the victim of inappropriate contact. She wouldn't fail now.

They made the transfer. He looked delighted as Charlotte first sniffed him and then curled up in his lap purring. "She likes me!"

Liz smiled. "Of course she does. She's clearly a good judge of character." A little flattery might nudge Dr. Collins toward taking a chance, and get Charlotte a new home.

Liz stood and hefted her computer bag. "Well, I'm glad this trip wasn't entirely wasted for you. I'll leave you two to get acquainted." She slipped away while Dr. Collins held a one-sided conversation with Charlotte. Liz dropped her empty mug and plate by the barista counter and headed for the door.

She had a vague impression of a man standing outside

looking in. That wasn't surprising, what with all the cats visible through the window. She didn't pay much attention, since she was in a hurry to escape while Dr. Collins was distracted. Liz stepped outside, her thoughts already elsewhere.

"Hello," the man said.

Liz stopped and looked over at William. "Oh. You."

"Good morning." He smiled, looking disgustingly cheerful—no doubt at the way he'd lulled her into a false sense of security the day before and then torpedoed Jade's plans. "I'm glad I found you," he added.

Liz put her hands on her hips. "Are you following me?"

"Er ... no?"

"Are you asking me? Because it sure looks like you are."

William blinked a couple of times. "Um. No. That is, I saw your car." He gestured vaguely down the street. "Carl said you took off this morning before they realized you were leaving, and, um." He shrugged. "I had thought you might want to see Sausage before you went to work."

A pang of guilt hit Liz. Granted, Sausage was more Jade's rescue than Liz's, but Liz hadn't even thought about the cat that morning. She'd been too wrapped up in her own anger, and ... well, if she had to admit it, which she would definitely not do aloud, she'd assumed Sausage was perfectly safe and happy at William's house. Keeping Sausage fed and safe from harm was a pretty low bar for decency, but William had already slithered under a pretty low bar. Who knew what nasty trick he'd play next?

"So ..." William shuffled his feet but smiled again, looking hopeful. "I was wondering if you wanted to have dinner out tonight?"

"Dinner. Tonight." Liz folded her arms. "With you."

He nodded. "I thought you might like a break from everyone. Well, from Caroline, specifically. She can be a lot. And ..." His gaze shifted past her shoulder, as if he couldn't be bothered to look her in the eyes while he talked to her. "I'd like to get to know you better. We could go somewhere quiet where we can talk." His cheeks were going red.

Liz was so angry her vision blurred. She had to take a couple of deep breaths before she could speak. "You want *me* to go out to *dinner* with *you.*"

His eyes widened as his gaze darted back to hers. "We don't have to go out. We could get takeout. Or I could cook? I just thought something quiet and private so we could talk."

Liz felt her smile stretch her cheeks until her teeth were bared. She almost wanted to thank William. She'd been keeping herself in check, but sometimes it felt like trying to keep the lava in a volcano.

And he'd just given her an excuse to explode.

Chapter 13

William wasn't great at reading expressions, but something about Liz's made him want to take a step back.

He wasn't sure where he'd gone wrong, but he tried to explain. "I know you're very busy with your dissertation. I certainly don't expect you to drop everything to spend time with me."

"Don't you?" The words came out through gritted teeth. "How generous."

"I thought you might occasionally like a break, and perhaps I could keep you company. Buy you a good meal."

"I don't need your charity."

"It would hardly be charity, since I'm asking for some of your precious time. And, uh …" William felt like he was racing downhill on a mountain bike with no breaks—with a deep gorge ahead—but he couldn't seem to stop talking. "I enjoy your company, and I thought perhaps you enjoyed mine. You seemed to, yesterday."

Liz got a thoughtful look and nodded. "You mean when I was using you as a chauffeur and borrowing a room of your house to nap while you did something else out of my sight? Yes, I suppose I did enjoy that."

When she put it that way … They really hadn't spent much time talking. Which was fine by him, but maybe she preferred a livelier companion. He could be lively, if he tried. Probably.

"That's a good point," he said. "We didn't get to know each other very well. I'd like to change that."

How could he convince her? Maybe he needed to let her know how impressive he found her.

"I don't like very many people," he said. "That first time we met, I desperately wanted to be anywhere else. But even in those circumstances, you intrigued me. I couldn't stop thinking about you afterward." Did that sound creepy and stalkerish? He cleared his throat. "Not that I'd—No doubt I'd have forgotten all about it soon."

She huffed out a short laugh and shook her head. Maybe he'd gone too far in trying to seem harmless.

He had to get Liz to see what she meant to him. He rushed onward with that same feeling of impending doom.

"But good fortune provided another opportunity. Carl was the one who asked me to look after you, yes, but I enjoyed the experience more than I expected. I liked being around you, even if we weren't talking all the time. Maybe more so because of that. Not that I don't enjoy hearing you talk—talking with you—"

He tried to put on the brakes before sailing off the cliff and plummeting into the gorge. "And now you're living right next door, and I have your cat in my spare bedroom, so I thought, why not get to know each other better?" He swiped the back of his hand across his forehead and it came away damp.

"Well, that's a very good question. Let me see if I can answer it." Liz lifted her chin. "First off, you don't like cats, and I can't tolerate anyone who doesn't like cats. Second, you told Carl not to give Jade the grant for her special needs cat rescue. I don't know if that's because you don't like cats, or if you don't want Jade spending more time with Carl, because you'd rather keep your best friend for yourself. Or possibly there are other reasons, equally despicable. I'm not interested in them, or you."

For a moment he could only stare. He knew he wasn't always in tune with other people, but how could his experience with Liz be so vastly different from hers with him?

Liz nodded once, as if his silence had confirmed her point. "So if there's nothing more, I'll be on my way, and I hope not to see you again unless it's to pick up Sausage." She started to turn.

"Wait." He reached for her arm but pulled back at her glare. "Please allow me to apologize. And maybe I can clarify a few things. I like cats."

She scoffed. "Sure, your behavior screams cat lover."

"I'm very allergic to them. I'm a little bit allergic to dogs as well, but I can manage that. I can be around cats if I take my allergy medicine first, but I wasn't expecting the cat café visit. I was also annoyed at having to spend time with Caroline, and frustrated because I didn't know how to handle that. I can see how it might have seemed like I was a cat hater, but I promise you it's not true."

She eyed him suspiciously, not speaking, but at least she wasn't leaving.

He took a deep breath and went on. "As for Jade's cat rescue, I'm not opposed to it in the least. I told Carl he'd have to postpone the grant, because the food pantry suffered a lot of storm damage. I thought providing services to people was more important than immediately rescuing more cats. I can see how others might disagree."

He attempted a smile. "In fact, I generally prefer the company of animals to people."

Her expression didn't change.

"But in any case," he said, "Carl is determined to give Jade a grant as soon as enough funds are freed up. I certainly won't try to stop him. I didn't want to stop him this time, but it's not really my decision. I was merely the messenger."

He considered saying something about not shooting the messenger, but he didn't want to give Liz any ideas.

"We are already working the numbers to see when we can make a new grant happen," he added.

"I thought your family was rich. Don't you have ..." She waved her hand vaguely. "Millions of dollars or something?"

"Well, the family is worth millions, on paper. That doesn't mean we have instant access to all that money. Some of it is tied up in the family businesses or property. Charitable donations come from an investment fund. If we give away too much at once, there won't be money left to earn more money so we can give away more money." That sentence had gotten away from him.

He cleared his throat. "If we only needed a few thousand dollars, we could do that now with our own money. Carl and I, I mean, we could come up with several thousand. But Jade needs a location, equipment, money for vet bills, and so on. Not to mention a modest salary if she's going to do this full time. Jade can't open her rescue without at least twenty thousand dollars startup, and the assurance that more is coming on a regular basis, so it didn't seem practical to make small donations now."

"Oh. I guess, but ..." Liz frowned. "Didn't her proposal cover all that?"

"Most of it, but she missed some things. That's why our charitable foundation has experts like Nash who can make sure causes aren't only worthy, but can actually succeed. She can use the delay to scout for locations and set up accounts with suppliers. We can get volunteers started on building the website and setting up social media accounts, so when her rescue opens, we'll have volunteers, fundraising, and publicity in place. Realistically, she couldn't expect to open for a few months anyway."

Liz stared at him for a while. He resisted the urge to speak. Usually it was easy not to speak, but for some reason she made him want to ramble. He'd probably given far more detail than necessary on the funding.

Finally she said, "Nobody told me that part. About the food pantry. Or that you were hoping to give Jade a grant in the future."

"So you assumed the worst."

Liz winced, but he hadn't meant it as criticism. He'd clearly bungled this badly. He found Liz interesting because she was outgoing, clever, and confident. She spoke her mind. Why should he assume someone like that would be interested in him? He'd barely participated in dinner conversation the night before, leaving the chatter to people who had more to say.

If he didn't believe his own thoughts were interesting, why would anyone else want to hear them?

And if that weren't bad enough, he'd sabotaged her friend's happiness. He hadn't meant to, but that wasn't an excuse.

He swallowed, his throat tight and his skin itchy with misery. "I'm glad we had a chance to clear up some things. I apologize again for not being clear in the first place, and for assuming you might ..." He didn't know how to put it. "Want to spend additional time with me."

She made an odd noise in her throat. It reminded him of the low whine the little beagle made when it seemed to want something but hadn't yet decided what. That didn't make any sense for Liz though.

"I won't bother you anymore now," he said. "Or ever, if you would prefer it that way. But I would like—I would take it as a very great kindness—if you would give me a chance to show you I can be a decent person. Not now, but later. When things settle down."

She gulped and nodded. That was something.

"Of course you can call on me if you ever need help of any kind," he said. "No strings attached! If you need a ride, I'm happy to give you one and won't bother you with conversation. I'm good with silence."

Not that she'd know that by this conversation. He felt like he'd talked more in the last ten minutes than the previous week. He needed to wrap up and get out of there before he dug himself a deeper hole.

"Thank you for giving me the chance to explain. I hope the rest of your day is much better." He clamped his mouth shut, nodded once, and hurried down the street, resisting the urge to look back.

He reached his car, parked in the city lot near hers. Liz was coming down the sidewalk toward the lot. He quickly backed out and turned to leave from the rear entrance, so she wouldn't be forced to acknowledge him again—or refuse to acknowledge him, which he didn't want to see.

He couldn't have made a bigger mess of that if he'd tried. For the first time in ages, he'd been interested in a woman, and he'd made so many poor choices that she couldn't stand him.

What was wrong with him? Had he gotten so used to being borderline rude to Caroline, who wouldn't take a hint, that he couldn't behave decently with other women? Had his family name and money gone to his head, despite his attempts to be ordinary, so he assumed all he had to do was crook a finger and the woman of his choice would come running? Or was he simply incapable of having a romantic relationship?

No, he wouldn't believe that. The thought hurt too much. If he was making mistakes, he'd learn and do better. Maybe Liz would give him a second chance, if he earned it.

William went home and let the dogs into the yard. He sat on the porch steps and threw balls for the lab-retriever mix and the mutt. Rufus and the beagle wrestled on the grass, and the elderly poodle flopped down next to William with her head in his lap. He scratched her ears. The Chihuahua raced between all of them.

William had told the office he was going to work from home. That way he could supervise the dogs when they went out, and two of the owners planned to pick up their dogs later. He'd also wanted to be available if Liz needed him for anything. So much for that idea.

At least the dogs liked him.

He didn't think he'd get any work done with so much else on his mind. No matter, he had plenty of sick and vacation days built up. He might not be sick, but it definitely hurt as he picked apart his conversation with Liz sentence by sentence, as near as he could remember it. Unfortunately, that didn't lead to an epiphany about what he should do next.

He needed advice. He'd normally talk to Carl, but Carl had his own problems. Jade would have plenty of insight into Liz, but asking her for advice would be like asking her to be on his side, when she was Liz's best friend. In any case, Carl and Jade were ... not part of the problem, exactly, but closely tied together with Liz and the misunderstandings. It felt like a breach of privacy to ask them for advice about this.

He would like a woman's opinion though. Not that he thought they were all the same—Caroline was the last person he'd ask for any insight into Liz—but the right woman might help him figure out where he'd gone wrong and how to make it better.

So who was the right woman?

Cheyenne, his cousin Nash's wife, was smart and sensible. She was also a cat lover. She ran Big Cat Rescue, but she liked felines of all sizes. And she'd worked through a big misunderstanding with Nash.

Once the dogs were worn out enough, William ushered them back inside and headed to Big Cat Rescue.

Chapter 14

Liz had thrown a grenade and found it tossed back in her face. Not that William had exploded. He'd just told her she was the one who started the war.

She groaned. Everything she'd thought she'd known had been twisted around. She didn't *like* to be wrong.

And she probably owed William, and maybe Carl, an apology.

But that could wait. She needed time to process what she'd learned. But before she did that, she needed to …

Right, she'd been on her way to campus, fired up to do battle. If the last five minutes had taught her anything, it was that she should avoid jumping to conclusions and especially avoid saying anything out loud about them. But the battle over her dissertation had been going on for ages. Liz had let herself be pushed around because she'd felt like she had no choice. Refusing Dr. Collins had reminded her that she did have choices. She had to get out of the PhD trap while she still had some shreds of self-worth.

Liz headed toward her car. She had a fifteen-minute drive to campus in which to find that fury again. Once she'd tackled the next battle, she could think about what William had said.

Her second advisor was in his office, kicked back in his desk chair with the computer mouse resting on one thigh and a giant travel mug on the other, no doubt filled with diet cola as usual. She knocked on his open door.

"Hey, Liz." His eyebrows went up when Liz closed the door behind her. "You look serious. What's up?"

She sat across from him. "I need your help. And Benjie—" She gave him a stern look. "I need actual *help*, not sympathy or suggestions that I need to relax more and not let things get to me."

A pained look flashed across his face, but he tipped his chair forward. He put the mouse and drink on his desk, leaned on his elbows, and focused on her. "I'm listening."

Liz made her case that she should defend the last version of her dissertation, the one that was at the proofreading stage before Dr. Bennett decided she needed to re-envision the whole thing. In many ways, Benjie was the opposite of Dr. Bennett. He'd done impressive research earlier in his career, but now he seemed to be coasting on that reputation. He gave his grad students a lot of freedom, and occasionally one of them did some groundbreaking work, which got Benjie's name added to another published paper.

His laissez-faire attitude—which Dr. Bennett called sheer laziness—wasn't what Liz was looking for in a mentor either, since the whole point in having a mentor was to get guidance, but with him on her side she might be able to stand up to Dr. Bennett.

Liz finished and waited. She perched on the edge of her chair, her neck and shoulders tight with tension. She gazed at Benjie, hoping he'd see her serious intent and decide, for once, that he'd rather fight Dr. Bennett than Liz.

"Okay," he said with a sigh. "You're right. I'm behind you."

Liz went lightheaded and almost slid out of the chair. She managed to smile. "I'd really rather have you *beside* me. Benjie, I need to know you won't back down if I tell Dr. Bennett I'm going to defend this semester. No deferring to her, no telling me to be patient. I'm tired of being at her mercy just because no one else will stand up to her."

He winced. "Point taken. I promise, I'll have your back on this one."

"Thank you." Liz stood, still shaky. "I'll talk to her … soon." Maybe she should've talked to Dr. Bennett first. The relief at having an ally meant the anger was draining out of Liz. Could she get away with hiding for the rest of the day and avoiding further confrontation?

Benjie got up and came around the desk as she opened

the door. "Well, it's always a pleasure to see you, even if you're asking me to do something."

"I really appreciate the help. I have to get out of here before I have a breakdown—in the clinical sense, not just a metaphor." She stepped through the door.

Dr. Bennett was storming down the hall. "Ms. Boyd! What have you done?"

Liz and Benjie exchanged panicked glances. Some people called Dr. Bennett a witch, but no one had suggested she had psychic powers or could hear through walls.

The woman planted herself in front of Liz, hands on hips. "I just got a message from Dr. Collins with a picture of his new cat! He said you'd suggested he adopt her!"

"Oh?" Liz wasn't sure why that was a problem. Dr. Bennett always seemed to see animals as research subjects, so maybe she thought no serious scientist had time for a pet. In that case, she ought to be glad Charlotte might sabotage Dr. Collins's work.

She tried to look innocent. "He said he wanted companionship at home. A cat seems like a good option."

Dr. Bennett leaned forward, gaze narrowed. "He thanked me for introducing you even though you turned down the postdoc position."

Liz's thoughts on cats fled. She didn't waste time on annoyance. Dr. Collins probably hadn't even heard her request for secrecy, because he was too busy hearing himself talk.

"You were supposed to get in his office so you could tell me how he gets those big grants!" It was a good thing Dr. Bennett didn't actually have superpowers, or she'd be shooting flames from her eyes.

Liz sucked in a breath. She might be about to ruin everything, but she was at the point where burning it all down sounded better than living this way. "I'm sorry, but I wouldn't do that even if I took the position. I'm a scientist, not a spy. If I take a postdoc position, my new employer will have my loyalty. It wouldn't be ethical to report anything to you."

"Ethical!" Dr. Bennett sputtered.

Benjie had backed into his office, but at that he stepped forward and echoed, "Ethical!" He grinned at Dr. Bennett. "That's right. It wouldn't be ethical of Liz, and it wasn't ethical of you to ask. You certainly wouldn't want the science community—or the University regents—to find out you made such a request."

Liz looked back at Dr. Bennett, whose face was bright red. "I didn't—She misunderstood—Anyway, Liz is *my* student!"

"Not for much longer," Liz said, going in for the kill. "I have a perfectly good dissertation draft already. I'm going to set a date for my defense before the end of this semester, using the data we have from last year."

Dr. Bennett glared at her, mouth working as if chewing on something too hard to swallow. Liz stared back. She couldn't show the slightest weakness.

"Yes, Liz and I were just discussing that," Benjie said cheerfully. "I trust that you will give her your full support. After all, it's our responsibility to see that our students get all the help they need in achieving *their* goals."

Dr. Bennett shifted her glare to Benjie and back to Liz. After a few seconds, she turned and marched down the hallway, head high.

Benjie chuckled softly. "Well done. She won't admit she was wrong, but she won't stand in your way now. She understood the threat."

Liz still wasn't sure *she* understood what had happened, except that it seemed like she'd be able to defend her dissertation in another month or two. And she didn't have to gear herself up to confront Dr. Bennett. Good thing, since she was as shaky as a newborn kitten.

"Thanks," she said.

Benjie patted her shoulder. "I'm closing the door. I need to recover from that, and I wouldn't want anyone to see me swoon."

Liz headed for the nearest exit. She still had a lot to do, but if she could just go home and collapse for an hour—

Oh, wait. She didn't have a home. She had a very generous man offering her a room as long as she needed one, and another man she'd misjudged. Well, darn. The day wasn't over yet.

William pulled up to Big Cat Rescue and went in to ask for Chey. Fifteen minutes later, he was holding metal fence rails in place while she fastened them to the posts. Chey was a few years older than William, lean and fit from a job that included hauling pails of meat out to the tigers and lions—and, apparently, building fences herself.

William looked past their section of fence. It took a moment before his eyes focused on the cougar watching him. "That animal is in a separate pen, right?"

"Of course. We don't put animals in enclosures we haven't finished building."

"Just checking." If he squinted he could see the top line of the fence that ran along the mountain lion's enclosure. With the tall grasses and native plants, it wasn't obvious. A trickle of fear ran down his spine as the golden eyes blinked at him, his primitive lizard brain reacting to danger. The animal was beautiful, muscles rippling under the golden skin of its shoulders as it shifted forward, nose twitching as if catching his scent in the breeze.

Chey brushed her hands on her jeans. "So what's up? You look like a man who has something on his mind— other than being stalked by a mountain lion, that is."

Stalked? William glanced at the cougar again. Had it moved? It didn't matter. They were on opposite sides of the fence.

He focused on Cheyenne "Yeah. I need some advice."

"Great. I like telling people what to do."

William explained the situation with Liz.

"I think I met her," Chey said. "She's studying animal intelligence—worms—right?"

"Yeah. She's smart, like you. And she loves cats, but I have to keep my distance from them. I figured you knew something about that."

Chey nodded. She and Nash had been college sweethearts until she took off for Asia to work on big cat conservation. Nash had a fear of cats, which he'd hidden by pretending he just didn't like them. Nash had eventually gotten therapy for his fear and later helped start the rescue hoping to lure Chey back home. It had worked.

Maybe he should be talking to Nash.

"You're communicating now, which is good," Chey said. "And you don't actually dislike cats."

"If the best that can be said about me is I don't dislike cats, I'm doomed."

She laughed. "You're handsome and nice. Rich, too, but I know you don't want to use money to attract a woman."

His face heated. "I didn't come here for compliments."

Chey squeezed his arm. "You can still have them. I guess the question is, what are you going to do to bridge the gaps between the two of you? If cats are really the issue—and you haven't quite convinced me they are—you know there are allergy shots, right?

He winced. He wasn't afraid of needles. He just didn't like them much. "I looked into it once, but it takes years."

"You won't get there if you don't start."

He sighed. "Okay, I'll make an appointment with an allergist. What else? I can hardly ask her to wait five years for me to get through allergy shots."

"Nash and I reunited after fifteen years apart. But yeah, it's not ideal, and you're starting from a different place."

"Come to think of it, I've had a cat in my house—just in one room—for the last couple of days. I've been able to manage my symptoms with allergy medicine. So I guess I could live with a cat or two, if they could be confined to certain areas."

Chey looked amused.

William's face got hotter. "And that's really getting ahead of myself."

"Yeah. You don't have to invite her to move in. Start slow and see what happens. If you like each other, you can find ways to compromise."

"That's a big if. Why should she even give me a chance?"

"She might not, and then you'll know she's not right for you. But she might. And like with the shots—"

"I won't get there if I don't start somewhere."

"Exactly. Now grab that next fence post."

Chapter 15

Liz sat in her car while she checked email and messages—and delayed figuring out what to do next. George had messaged asking if she wanted to get together. How long had it taken him to message her? It seemed like weeks but it was actually only two days. Not bad, neither desperate nor indifferent. It would be pleasant to spend time with someone so friendly and easygoing, even if he was part of the reason she'd misjudged William. In fact, it was nice to know she wasn't the only one to be misled by William's stuffy manner.

She deserved a break after her dramatic morning, didn't she? She wasn't up for anything as formal as a date though. Better to keep it casual while she figured out what she wanted. She messaged back that she'd be at the cat café later that afternoon. She'd have to see about getting a monthly pass if she was going to spend so much time there, but she couldn't think of any place better to be at the moment. Dr. Collins must be gone by now. Liz could get a bowl of soup for lunch and maybe something sweet as her reward for getting through her confrontations with Dr. Collins and Dr. Bennett.

As for her confrontation with William, she probably deserved a diet of bread and water while cats used their claws to climb up her legs. She'd been ready to assume the worst without enough data, and as a scientist, she should know better. Good thing most people didn't get what they deserved in life.

In any case, she could relax at the café, a place where she was highly unlikely to run into Dr. Bennett or William, the people she most wanted to avoid at the moment.

Although William had been outside the café that morning ... But most likely he'd simply been passing by.

What if he passed by again? Well, she could sit away from the window, so he wouldn't be likely to notice her, and even if he did notice her, no way would he come in to talk to her after the way she'd treated him. Which was good, because she wasn't ready to see him again. It was one thing to know she'd been mistaken, and another entirely to have to humble herself in front of someone chilly and aloof like William. Not that he'd been so cold lately. Not since their first meeting, really.

She shook her head and started the car. She definitely needed a relaxing afternoon and a break from thinking about everything.

But first she'd go to Big Cat Rescue to talk to Cheyenne about volunteering there. Liz was determined to have more time for her own interests, and by volunteering at the wild cat rescue, she'd meet interesting people, get to spend time with large cats, and have something special on her resume. How could you beat that?

As Liz drove up the long driveway to Big Cat Rescue, another car was coming out. She didn't pay that much attention to car styles, but this one looked familiar. Sunlight glared on the windshield, but then the angle shifted and for a moment she met the driver's eyes.

William? Here?

Liz jolted and her car swerved slightly. She forced her attention back on the road, slowed down, and pulled into an empty parking spot. She watched in her rearview mirror until the other car disappeared.

She'd never seen William in her life until the past week, and now he was everywhere! Okay, maybe they'd crossed paths before and she hadn't noticed him, but wasn't he supposed to be something of a hermit? And she definitely should have been safe going to a cat rescue of any kind. Even if he didn't hate them, they weren't his favorite animal.

It was just too weird. Had he been there to warn Cheyenne not to let Liz volunteer?

No, that was a paranoid idea. William couldn't have guessed she even wanted to volunteer, let alone that she was heading there on that day. In any case, she had to stop assuming the worst about him. He'd already proven her wrong.

It was still a weird coincidence.

He didn't appear to be coming back, so Liz headed into the rescue where a young woman—not Cheyenne—greeted her.

"Welcome! Feel free to look around and let me know if you have any questions. If you want to tour the big cats, it's twenty-five dollars."

Ouch. The price was probably in line with other zoos and rescues, and it was for a good cause, but it still seemed like a lot.

"I was hoping to talk to Cheyenne," Liz said.

The young woman frowned. "I believe she's either making her rounds or in the vet clinic. Is she expecting you?"

"No." Because Liz hadn't thought to make an appointment, which was, in retrospect, obviously a better procedure. "I just wanted to ask about volunteering."

"Oh, we have an application on our website for volunteers. But it's actually quite competitive." She looked a little smug to have made the cut, even though she was merely working at the counter taking money. "And new volunteers have to go through training sessions, so even if you get accepted, you might not get to start for months."

"Right. Of course." Maybe Liz should have quit trying to accomplish things while she was ahead. Or if not ahead, more or less even. It was tempting to slink away now and pretend she'd never been there.

The girl smiled. "If you want to take a tour, the next one starts in twenty minutes."

"Maybe." Liz glanced around at the posters and freestanding displays. It was a great little education center, with sections on various big cats, most of which were threatened or endangered, and their conservation.

She drifted closer to the section on mountain lions— also known as cougars, panthers, pumas, and catamounts, just to keep things interesting. They weren't the most popular big cat, or the most endangered, but they were a quintessential American cat. In a photo, the rescue's resident cougar stared at the viewer with tawny eyes and an expression that encouraged people to come closer as long as they wanted to end up as dinner. It was gorgeous, and also astonishing that anyone thought it would make a good pet, but all the animals here had been rescued from circuses, small roadside zoos, animal trainers, or individuals who thought it would be cool to have a lion or tiger cub—until the animal grew up.

Liz really did want to see the big cats, even if she had to spend her coffee money and wouldn't have a chance to talk to Cheyenne. Maybe she couldn't change all aspects of her life in one day, but touring the place would be a way of admitting what she wanted, if only to herself. Animal intelligence was fascinating, but the research wasn't about getting answers for her dissertation. It was about understanding these remarkable creatures better, finding ways to help them, and maybe even finding ways of understanding and helping people too.

The door opened and a family with three kids came in, the children running forward to look at displays.

Liz went back to the counter and pulled out her wallet. "I'll take the tour." She'd better keep her free lodging for a while if she was going to be spending money on tours, cat cafés, coffee, and sweets.

The tour guide was an older woman, probably a volunteer enjoying her retirement. She didn't rush the group, giving them plenty of time to look and ask questions, but the tour still moved too quickly for Liz. She could have watched a single animal for an hour. They all had large enclosures with open spaces, trees, ponds, and areas to hide, so each tour group saw something different depending on the day and their luck.

When their group passed the mountain lion enclosure, it was barely visible on the far side, blending in with the tan grasses. Liz would have liked to see it up close, but the experience was still impressive. Imagine being that close to a mountain lion and not knowing it was there! It was easy to see how that could happen to hikers.

In contrast, the lions were out and wrestling with each other. "These cubs were rescued from a small backyard zoo when they were six months old," the guide explained. "Since they were bred in captivity, they can't be released back into the wild, but here they have almost two acres of natural landscape instead of a small cage with a cement floor, and they get fresh meat every day."

They weren't yet full grown, so they were still rambunctious. They batted each other's heads with their paws, rolled in the grass, and bit lightly at each other's heads and necks. At one point, a cub rolled on its back, and when the other pounced, the first cub rabbit-kicked at his head.

"Will they stay together forever?" someone asked.

"They'll stay together unless they start showing behavior that would make them dangerous to each other," the guide said. "They're siblings, but they've been spayed and neutered. That should prevent the male from getting too aggressive, and of course we don't want to breed any of these animals, especially siblings."

They moved on to the leopards. Those had come from another sanctuary, one that didn't have the space and resources for them. All the enclosures had two fences, one to keep the animals in and another six feet away to keep people from getting too close to the main fence. The leopards were visible but about fifty feet away, lounging on the grass in the spring sun. Liz wished she had binoculars. She'd bring some next time, because there would definitely be a next time.

The tour circled back toward the education building. Liz was hungry for lunch but also more relaxed than she'd felt in ages. How could watching animals that could kill you with a swipe of a paw be so calming?

"Now we have a treat," the guide said. "Here's our director, Cheyenne, to feed the tigers!"

Liz's stomach growled loudly. People glanced at her.

"I'm not interested in stealing the tiger's food, I promise," Liz said. "And I certainly wouldn't try to eat a tiger!"

That got the little kids giggling. They all moved to the tiger enclosure. Cheyenne strode over with a metal pail. As the guide introduced her, Cheyenne scanned the group, smiling. When her gaze landed on Liz, her eyebrows rose. And had her smile faded? Liz smiled back anyway and gave a little wave.

The guide finished her introduction, and Cheyenne took over. "I'm going to go into the risk zone between the outer and inner fences. Only people who are trained to work with the big cats can do this. these are still wild animals, not pets!"

She entered the passage that surrounded the enclosure and hooked the outer gate behind herself. "Pari! Aanya! Time for lunch."

A tiger rose from the grass thirty feet away and padded closer. The sun shone on its orange fur striped with black and the white fur surrounding its face almost glowed. Despite its size, surely several hundred pounds, it made no sound moving across the short grass. Its lifted head was the height of Cheyenne's shoulder. It made a low moaning sound and then yawned, revealing three-inch-long yellowish canine teeth on the upper and lower jaws.

"Come on, Pari!" Cheyenne called. "You don't want your sister to get all the food."

Liz scanned the enclosure for the second tiger. She spotted it as it stood up from a shallow pond. It ran over to the fence, water droplets sparkling as they flew off its damp belly fur. A tremor went through her at the sight of a tiger running toward them. Her brain knew the fences were there, but her body wasn't 100% sure this was a safe and sensible place to be.

Cheyenne shared facts about the tigers as she tossed large chunks of beef over the fence. Aanya laid down with a meat-covered bone and licked it. Liz felt a simultaneous desire to rub the thickly furred ears and to back away from the powerful jaws.

Cheyenne answered questions as the animals ate. Then the guide said the tour had ended, but they were welcome to keep looking around the educational center and gift shop.

Liz hesitated as the group started back toward the main building. She wasn't sure what to say to Cheyenne now, but it felt odd not to say anything. She settled on, "Hello. Nice to see you again."

Cheyenne nodded once. "You too." The guide glanced back, and Cheyenne said, "It's okay, I'll walk back with her."

Liz wasn't sure whether to be grateful or nervous that she got to spend a few minutes with the rescue's director after all.

Cheyenne turned back to Liz. "I'm surprised to see you here today."

Liz tried to come up with an answer. "Today specifically? I mean, that you're surprised to see me. Or just in general?"

"I guess I'm not surprised to see you in general. Today is a coincidence."

What did that mean?

Cheyenne was with Nash, who was William's cousin. William had just been here. Regardless of why he'd come, he'd likely visited with his cousin's wife. Maybe he had said something about Liz—and if so, it probably hadn't been anything good. Talk about burning bridges. Liz's poor judgment of William might have cost her not only his friendship, but some professional connections too.

Liz gulped. "You didn't happen to talk to William today, did you?"

Cheyenne shook her head, but before Liz could relax,

she said, "I'm not getting in the middle of anything."

Oops. Liz decided not to follow up on that. "I actually came out to ask about volunteering. I'll fill out a form. Unless ..." *Unless there's no point because you're mad at me for how I treated William.*

"Yes, please start with the paperwork," Cheyenne said. "You know, we have a lot of people wanting to volunteer, so we have some pretty strict guidelines."

Liz's heart sank. "I realize you'd be doing me a favor and not the other way around."

"It's twelve hours a month minimum. Do you think you'd be able to manage that with your PhD work?"

Liz's heart considered rising again. Maybe Cheyenne wasn't holding a grudge after all. She might merely be worried that Liz couldn't handle her PhD and volunteer hours as well, which wasn't unreasonable.

"I talked to my advisors this morning," Liz said. "I'm hoping to defend in about a month. Then I'll have more free time, although I guess I don't know where I'll find work." Her heart decided sinking was the right option. "You probably don't want to train me if I can't commit to being here awhile."

"That's true." Cheyenne studied Liz for a few seconds. Liz had no idea what was going through the other woman's mind. Finally Cheyenne said, "Fill out the paperwork anyway. Maybe by the time we're ready to train a new volunteer group you'll know what you're doing and where you'll be."

Liz's heart was getting quite a workout with the ups and downs. She grinned at Cheyenne. "I'll do that. Thank you."

They started walking back toward the main building. After a moment, Liz added, "By the way, you were completely right about giving William a second chance. I misjudged him."

Was it Liz's imagination, or did Cheyenne's posture relax at that? "He'll be glad to hear that," she said.

Liz nodded. Wait—that comment might have been a pointed suggestion that Liz needed to tell William she'd misjudged him. Which she did need to do. But Cheyenne had said she didn't want to get involved, so maybe Liz should keep her mouth shut.

They reached the building. Liz's stomach grumbled again. "I'm going to take off now." She hesitated and then decided to go for it. "Unless you'd like to join me for lunch?"

"Not today. But maybe one day soon."

"Great. I'll be in touch." Liz headed for the parking lot. Maybe she hadn't burned all of her bridges here after all.

Chapter 16

Well, Liz had accomplished a lot that day. Surely she deserved to take the rest of the day off!

Except she still owed William an apology. She could text him ... But that seemed like a copout. She'd screwed up, so she should own up to it. Grow up, stand up, and give up her wounded pride.

That was too far *up* for her at the moment. She'd probably see him that evening at Carl's house. She'd pull him aside and apologize for misjudging him. Although if he'd communicated better it might not have happened!

She drove back to the cat café. One of these days she'd have to get some groceries so she could make lunches. Was it fair to take up space in Carl's refrigerator? Ugh, being a houseguest was challenging. She'd better get the rest of her rent money refunded so she could spend it on eating out.

Liz parked in the city lot and walked through the sunshine to the café. It was hard to believe they'd had an enormous storm a couple of days before. That was spring weather for you.

At the café, she peered through the window to make sure Dr. Collins was gone. It looked safe. A half dozen people were petting or playing with cats. Liz didn't recognize any of them.

Inside, she ordered the lunch special: a bowl of vegan minestrone with a fresh baked roll and a cup of coffee. That put her right at the amount she needed to pay in order to get access to the cat lounge.

The barista, a tattooed young woman, scooped soup from a big pot.

Liz said, "When I was here earlier, there was another customer. A tall man, bald on top. It sounded like he wanted to adopt Charlotte."

The woman nodded. "He filled out an application. Approval takes a few days."

"I think they'll be a good fit." Liz carried her lunch into the cat room. It was pretty quiet, with only a pair of older women chatting with each other and everyone else focused on their food or the cats. Liz settled at an empty table. A large, long-haired black cat jumped down from a cat tree and strode across the padded bench with its nose twitching like a predator scenting prey. It stopped two feet from Liz.

"Really, minestrone?" she asked it. "I can see going for fish chowder, but noodles and vegetables?"

The cat sat, stared at her for a few seconds, and then began grooming, licking a paw and rubbing it over its head. As she ate, Liz shot glances at the cat, which seemed to ignore her. When she finished her soup and roll, she leaned back with her coffee in one hand and slowly held her other hand out to the cat. It blinked at her a couple of times and finally stretched forward to sniff her hand. She gave it half a minute before she tried to pet the animal. It pushed its head into her hand and purred.

Liz smiled. "Yeah, you might not be a panther, but a panther wouldn't let me do this, would it?"

"I guess we're both popular with cats."

Liz glanced up at George. She'd been so focused on the cat she hadn't noticed him come in. "Hi."

He pulled out a chair and sat down. "How are you? Man, it's been a week. That storm really tore up my yard. I had to get a crew in to take care of a tree that was falling down."

"It was rough," Liz said. "I heard it did a lot of damage to the food pantry, and—"

"Places all over town were hit." George leaned back and grinned at her. "And guess what? You'll never believe it. I heard ol' Will took in a pack of homeless dogs. Can you imagine?"

"Very well," Liz said. "That reminds me, you said William's dog bit you. When was that?"

He shrugged. "Long enough ago for the wound to scar.

And not just on the outside, you know? That kind of thing stays with you."

He was still making it sound like it was recent. Liz tried to channel Jade's faith in humanity and find the most positive interpretation. Trauma affected people in different ways, so maybe it was recent to him.

"I can imagine," Liz said. "Plenty of people are afraid of dogs because they were bitten by one—"

"Hey, I'm not *afraid* of dogs! I just don't like people who don't control their dogs properly."

"Right. But the thing is, I met William's dog. It's pretty hard to imagine Rufus biting you."

"Oh, no, not Rufus. This was another one." George's gaze narrowed. "When did you meet Will's dog? You haven't been hanging out with him, have you?"

Liz hesitated. How could she even answer that question? *Hanging out* wasn't the term she'd use, but she'd spent a surprising amount of time with him— especially when you considered that she hadn't planned to ever see him again.

George shook his head. "Why are we talking about Will and his dogs anyway? We're in a cat café—don't want to make the cats jealous!" He chuckled. "Speaking of, where's my favorite little lady?"

He stood up and looked around, then went to a window hammock where he scooped up Lydia. The café rules said not to pick up any cats, for their safety and the customers', but George was walking back before Liz could say anything. Lydia yawned and stretched as George sat again.

"I figured she must be sleeping since she didn't greet me right away," George said. "You can really judge people by how they feel about cats and how cats feel about them, right? I mean, look at this!" Lydia was sprawled on her back as George rubbed her chest and neck. "How could anyone not think cats are the greatest?"

He launched into a story about—well, she wasn't really sure, as she'd stopped paying attention.

Liz couldn't believe she'd found George charming. He was trying too hard, which could be a sign of nerves, but he was also badmouthing William to make himself look better. And she didn't have the patience for someone who interrupted her and rambled. If she wanted that, she'd take the job with Dr. Collins.

Liz gave the black cat a last head rub and started collecting her things. "Well, I ought to get going."

"But I just got here! I haven't had a chance to ask you about your research." George leaned forward and smiled in a way that managed to be sad, pleading, and a bit flirtatious. "Here I thought I'd get to buy you coffee and dessert and hear about all the clever things you've been doing. Instead you finish your lunch before I even get here and now you want to leave? At least have something sweet before you go." The skin at the corners of his eyes crinkled as he smiled.

Liz hesitated. Maybe it was vanity to like George more when he took an interest in her work, but on the other hand, why would she want to hang out with a man who took no interest in her? Besides, she needed to stop jumping to conclusions. George might reward a second chance just as William had.

"I guess I have time for a coffee refill and maybe a cookie. It's not like I'm going to get a lot of work done today after everything that's already happened."

"Ooh, it sounds like you have a story I need to hear." George jumped up. "How about we share a piece of key lime poundcake? The bakers here are phenomenal."

"I can't say no to that." Liz followed him out to refill her coffee.

George chatted with the barista and left a good tip. They returned to the cat room with a thick wedge of poundcake and enjoyed its incredible sweet-tart lime flavor. Over the next hour of talking and laughing, Liz forgot why she'd found George annoying earlier. She really had to stop being so judgmental.

Finally George pulled out his phone. "Shoot, I have to run. But this has been fantastic. Let's do it again soon."

Liz found herself grinning back at him. He hurried out and she followed more slowly. She deposited her dishes by the barista station and pulled on her coat, glancing at the menu board. She could bring home some dessert as an apology and peace offering. "May I have ten of the cranberry pistachio biscotti, please?" she asked the barista.

With those in her bag, Liz headed out. When she pulled up to Carl's house, she saw his car and Jade's. William would walk over, which was nice for him but meant Liz had no idea if he'd be there or not. She entered the house—Carl had given her a key, but the front door was unlocked—and paused, listening. No voices, though she did hear music. She dropped off the biscotti in the kitchen and her computer bag in her guestroom. The music was coming from behind Caroline's closed door.

No William yet. Liz took a shaky breath. She wanted to see him, and she didn't. In any case, she had time to find out if she also needed to apologize to Carl, assuming his car meant he was here somewhere.

Liz found him and Jade on the back porch. They were sitting close together on a two-person swing, with half-full wineglasses in their hands and the bottle on a little table nearby. Must be a special occasion. Liz hesitated at the sliding glass door to the porch. They might not want to be interrupted. But she didn't know how much time she had before William arrived—or worse, Caroline came out and derailed the conversation. She slid open the door and stepped outside.

Carl smiled. "Grab yourself a glass and join us." How could some people be so nice all the time?

"What's that in your lap?" Liz asked Jade.

Jade held up a tiny ball of white fur. Liz might have

mistaken it for a fluffy pom pom if not for the little dark eyes and pink nose.

"Jellybean has a cleft palate," Jade kissed the small head.

"The roof of his mouth didn't close over, so he has to be fed by tube," Carl explained. "Otherwise the food would go up to his sinus cavity. He might choke or aspirate, and he wouldn't get any nutrition. Jade is so good at this."

Jade smiled warmly at Carl and then shifted her gaze back to Liz. "We might be able to get him surgery eventually, but for now he needs a lot of care, and I'm the lucky gal who gets to take care of him."

The kitten made a tiny mew. It sounded demanding and also adorable. Liz's heart melted. "Let me know if you need help."

"Thanks." Jade gazed at the kitten with love. "I can handle him, but if you could keep checking on Sausage, that would help me."

"We're going to give him a bath later." Carl sounded like he'd never had such a treat.

"Lucky you." Liz perched on the edge of a chair. "I ran into William today."

"Oh? That's a little surprising." Carl grinned. "He generally avoids being seen by anyone except a few close friends. I guess you're becoming one of them."

Liz gulped. That seemed about as far from the truth as possible. But it sounded like William hadn't told Carl about her mistake, unless Carl was being nice by pretending he didn't know, and that much niceness was really too much for her to process.

Liz looked at Jade and back at Carl. "He said you're going to try to find the money for Jade's rescue in a few months."

"Absolutely! It hurts that we couldn't do it right away." He pressed a hand against his chest as if he actually felt pain there. "But I visited the food pantry today and things are dire. Or they would be, but fortunately we have the cash to buy new equipment, and the storm wasn't too widespread, so the whole region isn't full of people needing appliances and roofers. We got some restaurant vouchers to give out for the next few days until the pantry is back in action."

Jade was looking at Carl as if he'd personally saved all those people—which in a way, he had. Jade had clearly gotten over any disappointment that she'd have to wait for funding. She and Carl deserved each other.

"I'm glad to hear that," Liz said. "When Caroline told me William had insisted Jade couldn't get the money, I assumed the worst."

Jade frowned. "When was this? I told you last night about the delay."

"You told me you weren't getting the money. You didn't mention that you'd be getting it soon." Liz didn't want to criticize anyone—okay, she did, but she was trying to be subtle. "Then Caroline stopped in and implied William wouldn't let Carl give you the grant."

Carl sighed. "I'll speak to her."

"I'm sure it was only a misunderstanding," Jade murmured.

"It doesn't really matter at this point," Liz said. "I don't want to make waves." She wanted to give Carl a clue that Caroline might be trying to sabotage certain relationships, but she didn't think confronting Caroline would fix anything. "I'm just giving you a heads up, in case Caroline said anything to other people. And I want to apologize for misjudging you and William."

"No need to apologize," Carl said. "I can see how that was confusing."

Jade studied Liz. "You said you ran into William today. I gather he explained the situation."

Liz had known Jade long enough to interpret her look. It said, *You didn't do anything foolish, did you?*

Liz winced. "He explained after I yelled at him. I need to do more than apologize. I might need to grovel. Any suggestions for making amends?"

Jade shook her head at Liz. "Just talk to him. I'm sure William isn't the type to hold a grudge."

Carl didn't look so certain, and he knew William a lot better. "Do you want me to talk to him?"

"No, I made my bed, so I'll lie in it." If only that platitude had more to do with lying in actual beds. Liz would be happy to stay in bed for a week. An image filled her mind, Liz in bed looking up at William as she apologized and asked how she could make it up to him.

That was not a place she needed her mind to go.

Jade looked sympathetic. "Poor you. How about a glass of wine now?"

Of course Jade wouldn't even say, "I told you so." Maybe Liz should give them their privacy, but she couldn't resist the temptation of relaxing on the porch with a glass of wine and two lovely people. If William joined them, she could apologize to him without the humiliation of Caroline listening in. If he didn't, relaxing with a glass of wine would put her in a better frame of mind to go make her apologies.

Liz stood. "Absolutely. I'll grab a glass."

Chapter 17

William fed the remaining dogs. The lab-retriever mix and the Chihuahua had been reclaimed by their owners. That made William's life easier, as those were the two most likely to escape, the first by jumping over the fence and the second by squeezing through a gap. William hadn't found any gaps in his fence, but that didn't mean a tiny dog wouldn't squeeze through where it looked impossible.

It was quieter and a little lonely without those two.

William went out to the porch where Rufus and the poodle were waiting for their special diets. He distributed the food and sat on the steps watching them. Rufus's checked out Sadie's food. They play-nipped at each other, the poodle doing a little dance and Rufus wiggling his whole body. He'd seemed younger and more energetic since they'd had house guests. Rufus decided Sadie's food wasn't any better than his, and the two settled down to eat.

"You like having friends, don't you?" William said to Rufus. "We might get to keep Sadie."

The elderly poodle's people were moving in with family who had a new baby and didn't want a dog around. The owners had offered to sign Sadie over to William if he'd cover her medical care. They'd been struggling to make the payments on the dog's medicine even before their housing disaster. William had considered paying for Sadie's healthcare and letting the couple keep the dog, but it sounded like Sadie would be better off with him than the family that would keep her chained outside. It would be good for Rufus too—and for William. He'd thought he had everything he needed. Now it seemed he'd just been set in his ways.

"Hello!" The call came from the far end of his yard.

William looked over to see Liz waving as she came through the gate. His heart gave a little leap, like a puppy seeing a new friend.

She probably wanted to see Sausage. William had intended to stay in his office if he was home when Liz visited the cat. But it would seem weird to retreat now, wouldn't it?

And he wanted to see her, even if she didn't like him.

She strode toward him, her pace brisk. How did she seem to have more energy than most people? She had so many stressful things in her life, yet she faced them like a fighter, refusing to buckle under the weight. He'd like to remove some of that weight, but he also found her fighting spirit incredibly attractive.

Sadie and Rufus decided a visitor was more interesting than their diet food. Sadie pranced over to greet Liz and Rufus followed, his stubby tail and whole back end wagging.

Liz crouched and greeted the dogs. Sadie bumped into her and Liz fell back to sit on the ground. She laughed as Rufus tried to climb into her lap and Sadie licked her face. Liz didn't seem to mind grass stains and fur on her clothes or dog slobber on her cheek. William mentally added that to his list of qualities that made a woman attractive.

After a few minutes of wrestling and petting, the group joined William on the porch. Before he could get up, Liz sat on the steps beside him. "Hey."

"Hi. Um. I haven't fed Sausage yet if you want to do that."

"I do, in a minute." She took a deep breath and let it out. "But first I need to apologize. I was out of line this morning."

"You weren't, really." It felt good to hear her say that though. "It's my fault for acting like a jerk."

"But you didn't! Or at least …" She grabbed Rufus's jowly cheeks and gently shook them, her gaze on the dog. "I guess I interpreted some of your behavior that way, but I jumped to conclusions."

"They were reasonable conclusions. I have this bad

habit of holding conversations in my head and not realizing the other person wasn't part of them."

She glanced at him sideways, her lips curving in a way that did strange things to his insides. "Yeah, things would be easier if you included me in those conversations."

Something loosened in William's chest. Liz talked as if they would have more conversations in the future! Maybe he hadn't entirely screwed up his chances.

"I'll try." He fished around for a topic. "How was your day?"

"It was ... mixed." She told him about talking to her advisors.

"That all sounds good. Stressful in the moment, but good."

"Yeah, I think so. It wasn't easy, but I'm glad I did it." She worried her bottom lip with her teeth for a moment. "I also went to Big Cat Rescue."

"Right, I thought that was you." William's mind raced. Had Liz said anything to Cheyenne about him? Had Cheyenne said anything to Liz? Surely not. It wasn't like he was an exciting topic of conversation. He cleared his throat. "I'd been visiting Cheyenne."

"I talked to her too. I'm going to apply as a volunteer."

"That's great. I'm sure you'll enjoy it, and they'll be lucky to have you."

"I hope so." She focused on Rufus again, scratching behind his ear as he flopped to the porch and closed his eyes in ecstasy. "I probably can't start until after I defend my dissertation. Then I need to look for work, because I also turned down the position with Dr. Collins. So I don't know where I'll be in a few months."

That hurt more than it should have. William couldn't answer for a few seconds. Finally he managed, "I'm sure you'll find a great job. I hope it's one around here. Not that—I mean, I'm not—"

He should have stopped after the first sentence. It wasn't any of his business where she worked, and their friendship wasn't in a place where he could say he'd miss her if she left.

"I kind of hope it's around here too." Were her cheeks going pink? Or was that merely the slanting rays of the evening sun giving her a warm glow? "I'd miss Jade if I left, and I have other friends. Not that I see them often, but maybe I could in the future. I'm determined not to focus my whole life on my work."

He absolutely would not read anything into that. Of course she had other friends, and they didn't include him.

That reminded him. "Oh, I talked to your Mrs. Aguilar today."

"About the dogs? I noticed some seem to be missing."

"Two of them are inside, but two went home. Yeah, about that, but also about your building." He hesitated. Would she think he'd overstepped by getting involved? "I know you didn't ask me for help with it, but she did."

Liz stared. After about two seconds, she seemed to realize her mouth was open. She closed it and frowned. "I can't picture you fixing our roof."

That stung. "I'm capable of physical labor." He didn't know anything about fixing roofs, but that was beside the point. "But you're right, I'll leave that for the professionals. What I can do is help with the negotiations with the building owner."

Her frown turned into a scowl. "Right, because you're rich and important. Mrs. Aguilar and Mrs. Phen are doing a fine job of making sure the tenants get what they deserve."

"I'm sure, but you all need a good lawyer to review the contract—" He broke off because she'd put her hand over her face.

A moment later she dropped her hand and turned to look at him. "I'm sorry. I came over to apologize for jumping to conclusions, but apparently I'm still training for the conclusion jumping Olympics. It was nice of you to offer to help."

"I'm glad to do it." He kind of liked it when she called him on stuff too, but if he said that, he'd sound like ... He didn't even know what.

She studied him for a few seconds. "You know, in your way you might be almost as nice as Carl and Jade."

That forced a laugh out of him. "I doubt that."

"You just hide it a lot better. How am I surrounded by such nice people when I'm not one of them?"

"You're nice."

She shook her head. "I'm really not. I'm short-tempered, sarcastic, and usually too caught up in my own priorities to pay enough attention to other people. I'm trying to change that last part, but I don't know if I can change the temper and sarcasm."

He thought about that. "I'd say you're figuring out what you want and learning to set boundaries. That's not a bad thing."

"That's putting a positive spin on it. And it took me an awful long time to set boundaries with Dr. Bennett." She shook her head again. "Anyway. I didn't come here for compliments. I came to apologize, and I think I managed that, right?"

He nodded. "Apology accepted, of course."

Her smile looked hopeful as she held out her hand. "Friends?"

He took her hand. "Friends." They didn't exactly shake, simply holding and squeezing lightly for a moment. He didn't want to let go. But she'd said friends, nothing else. He kept his grip gentle until she pulled away.

Liz pushed to her feet. "I guess I should check on Sausage."

He stood as well and opened the door for her. They waited as the various dogs ran in and out, trying to figure out where the excitement would be.

"I was going to avoid Carl's place tonight," he said, "since you were mad at me, but maybe now ..." He waited for her reaction, studying her face so he'd see any suggestion of annoyance or disappointment.

She slipped past the dogs and stopped outside the room that held Sausage. She looked back at him with her hand on the door handle. "You know, I was thinking of giving Jade and Carl some privacy this evening. It's a nice night. I might walk into town and grab dinner, if you'd like to join me?"

Friends. She'd said they were friends. Still, he couldn't repress his grin. "That sounds perfect."

Spending the evening with William was surprisingly nice. At first he was clearly working at the conversation, but as long as Liz waited for a few seconds after asking a question or making a comment, he'd respond. Maybe he usually had conversations in his mind because other people rushed to fill the silences. But he was willing to share his thoughts out loud with a patient companion. Liz didn't consider herself particularly patient, but the reward was worth it. William wasn't the most exciting person she'd ever met, but he was intelligent and thoughtful.

Their quick dinner turned into a slow one, and by the time they headed back to William's neighborhood, it really did feel like a friendship. Liz glanced at his profile as they walked. He was classically tall, dark, and handsome, which she could take or leave, but his small, cautious smiles were little treasures.

"What are your plans for the rest of the evening?" he asked.

"Huh. I guess I don't have any."

The corner of his mouth twitched up. "You sound surprised."

"Kind of. I feel like I've had a very long, full day already." Liz thought for a minute. "I wouldn't mind spending time with Jade, but she and Carl seemed perfectly happy with each other's company this evening. I suppose I could try to distract Caroline on their behalf."

She and William exchanged wincing expressions. "I won't offer to help you with that," he said.

Liz laughed. "I see where your boundaries are. How did you and Carl get so close anyway? You're very different people."

"Maybe that's why. You and Jade are pretty different as well."

"Yeah. I guess optimistic sweethearts like them need people like us who are more ..."

"Pragmatic."

"I was thinking of misanthropic or at least suspicious of everyone."

"Tomato, tomahto," William said, and Liz snickered. They walked on in silence. William was several inches taller than Liz but had a more leisurely gait, so their pace was well matched.

After a minute, he said, "I know I'm lucky to have a friend like Carl. He's the most accepting, forgiving person I know, and I need someone who will forgive my foibles. I'm not particularly forgiving myself. Sometimes I wish I could be more like him, but this leopard's spots go deep. I hope Jade ..."

"You hope Jade what?" The breeze picked up, and Liz shivered a little as she waited for his answer. She tried hard not to jump to a conclusion but still tensed.

"I'm not sure how to put it. I don't want to say I hope she's worthy of him, because she could be amazing and still not right for him. I guess I'm wondering if she's as serious as he is."

Liz had started to bristle when it seemed like William might be criticizing her friend, but his last comment totally distracted her from that. "Is *he* serious?"

"Um. Maybe I shouldn't say."

Liz nudged William with her elbow. "Too late. If it helps, I'm pretty sure Jade is smitten."

"It does help. I don't know her well enough to judge." His eyebrows drew together. "I've never seen her not look happy, even after you two lost your apartment and she couldn't get the grant yet."

"Jade is chronically cheerful, maybe even pathologically cheerful, but she also really likes Carl. And she's not after his money or anything. Jade isn't like that."

"Good, because he's not rich."

Liz glanced over at him with raised eyebrows.

"Okay, he might be richer than Jade, or anyone who lived in your apartment building." William's smile was rueful. "I do realize there are plenty of people who aren't exactly poor but aren't middle-class either."

"Yeah, and Jade won't ever earn much working in animal rescue. But she loves it." Liz sighed. "I don't see riches in my future either, but I'll settle for a job that pays the bills and doesn't make me work evenings and weekends."

Wait, maybe she shouldn't have said that. They'd gotten so comfortable that she'd almost forgotten William was rich, or at least from a rich family. She didn't want him to think she was suggesting something. She didn't know what he might read into her statement, but anything would be bad.

She focused on the path ahead and tried to speak lightly. "I'm not after any man's wealth either. We're just trying to get by and maybe make a slight difference in the world, you know?"

He gave a rusty laugh. "That doesn't sound so misanthropic."

"Well, we are more focused on animals than people. I guess we could be misanthropic and, what would it be, zoophilic? Except humans are technically animals too."

"I guess we're the worst animals."

"Well ... I'm not crazy about mosquitoes. Or cockroaches. I could probably come up with a few dozen animals worse than humans."

He smiled. "Are we better or worse than worms?"

"Worse. Definitely worse."

They finished the walk in companionable chatter. For some reason—Liz didn't stop to examine it too closely—she felt compelled to take his arm as they maneuvered around a bulge in the sidewalk caused by a tree root. When they reached his gate, he opened it and guided her through with a light hand on her back. When he asked if she wanted a beer before heading back to Carl's, she agreed—to give Carl and Jade more time together. To avoid Caroline. Because she hadn't had an evening off in so long.

Or maybe just because she was enjoying William's company.

Chapter 18

Liz found the next couple of weeks surprisingly enjoyable. She worked hard, but finalizing the dissertation draft she already had was way easier than starting over. Since she didn't need new research, she even kept her lab time strictly to four hours a day, meaning she was almost making minimum wage with the grant money covering her that semester. Dr. Bennett managed to comment at least once a day that Liz should reconsider and base her dissertation on their new research plan, but Liz managed to ignore Dr. Bennett's grumbles.

Carl had spoken to Caroline, who sulked but didn't try to sabotage Liz's relationships again. Even better, Caroline spent more time away from the house. Evenings with Jade, Carl, and William were full of conversation and laughter. If Liz got tired of the lovebirds or if Caroline was home and pouting, Liz could head over to William's place to cuddle with Sausage, play with the dogs, or sit on the back porch with William and watch the sun set and the stars come out.

Her new friendships did have one downside. Now if Liz found a job far away, she'd not only lose Jade but also Carl and William. Not that she'd lose them entirely, but occasional visits wouldn't be the same.

Liz exchanged a few messages with George but kept it light, brief greetings and an occasional funny meme. He could be charming and fun, but she didn't want to give him the wrong idea. Liz didn't have the time or emotional energy for relationship and didn't think she'd want one with George anyway. Once she defended her dissertation, got her PhD, and had a job, she could think about the future.

She also ignored Jade and Carl's sly smiles when she headed over to William's. She and William were just friends, and Liz wasn't about to be sucked into dreaming of romance just because Jade and Carl were making heart-eyes at each other.

So what if sometimes Liz imagined kissing William? That just proved she wasn't dead.

And maybe they were going to mewvie night at the cat café as a foursome, but that didn't mean it was a date. Liz wasn't even getting dressed up, other than taking an extra minute to fuss with her hair. After all, any clothes would be covered with cat hair by the end of the evening, and dangling jewelry might attract playful feline predators.

Carl, Jade, and Liz were starting the evening with a glass of wine on the back porch. Liz just happened to notice when William's back door opened and he headed across his lawn, looking mouthwatering in jeans and a long-sleeved shirt open at the collar.

It wasn't like she'd been looking for him, particularly. And if she got up to meet him at the gate, that was merely so she could greet Rufus and Sadie. The other dogs had been collected by their people. Now Rufus and Sadie fawned over each other almost as much as Carl and Jade did.

It was almost sickening, really, being around so much lovey-dovey stuff.

Okay, it was actually very cute.

William rested a hand on the gate as Liz played with the dogs. She glanced up at him. "You sure you'll survive a couple of hours around cats?"

"It will be a good test. The allergist says this treatment should have made a difference already. It's been a full-day appointment each week, but if they're right, in another month I should be fairly desensitized."

"I should hope so given all the needles you've had to endure."

He shrugged. "It's worth it. If I'd known about the fast option, I might've done it years ago."

Liz stood and brushed off her jeans. "Does this mean you're thinking about getting a cat, or you're just happy to avoid the reaction when you come into contact with them?"

"I'm not sure yet." His smile was soft and sweet. "If nothing else, I can hang out with all you cat lovers without sneezing and coughing from the dander on your clothes. And I have been getting pretty attached to Sausage."

Liz's heart gave a little pang. She'd gotten awfully attached to Sausage as well. Granted, he distracted her from her work, demanding playtime or crawling into her lap and pushing his head up under her chin as he purred. But it turned out an occasional diversion wasn't the worst thing in the world. The cat reminded her to take breaks, getting up to move around or occasionally lying down for a quick catnap—although why short, light naps were called that, she didn't know. Sausage could zonk out for hours, sprawled across the bed snoring in faint little whistles.

But Sausage would be very lucky to be adopted by William, if William got to the point where he could cuddle Sausage without needing to change clothes and wash his hands and face immediately afterward. The cat had been introduced to the two dogs, and they all got along. Sausage was living like a king.

They joined Liz and Carl on the porch. Liz refused to let Jade catch her eye as she poured William a glass of wine.

"Where's Caroline this evening?" William asked.

"A fraternity party," Carl said. "She's been on the phone with some guy for hours. I met him. He's kind of a young idiot, but ..." Carl spread his hands.

"We all were once," William said. "I'm glad she's hanging out with people her own age."

They sipped wine and nibbled on a charcuterie board Jade had put together, something to fill them up a little so they wouldn't overindulge in the café's sweets. Liz let the conversation wash over her as she gazed out at the green and gold grasses, William's white house, and the evening sun lighting up distant clouds in pink and orange.

I could do this forever.

She shook off the thought. This wasn't her life. It was more like a wonderful vacation. But at some point she'd have to get back to the everyday grind.

They walked into town, since the cat café was only a little over a mile away. It was a nice night, and they'd avoid competing for parking.

"This should be fun," Jade said. "Cats are often more active at night, so I bet we'll have some playful kitties."

"I take it we're not expected to pay that much attention to the movie," William said.

Jade grinned at him. "Pay attention to whatever you find most interesting."

William glanced at Liz and quickly away.

They reached the café, where several people were already in line at the barista counter. The tickets they'd reserved ahead of time included a drink and a sweet for the evening in the cat room. When they reached the counter, they debated over the dessert options and decided to share between the four of them. They got a carrot cupcake with sour cream frosting, an almond coconut cupcake, butterscotch pecan cookies, and molasses cookies.

"That's my sugar for the week," Jade said.

"If you want, I'll eat your share," Liz said.

"Aw, you're so helpful!" Jade nudged her shoulder.

"That's me, a helper."

They went into the cat room. The chairs and tables had been shifted around so all the chairs faced a large screen. About twenty people were already there laughing and chatting and playing with cats.

One of them turned and Liz recognized George. Had she mentioned coming to the movie? Possibly. She vaguely recalled quickly answering a text about her weekend plans, noting she was busy. Had he come hoping to see her? That would be awkward. Of course he had every right to be there, but George and William had some kind of past conflict Liz hadn't figured out yet. It was easier when she could keep those two parts of her life separate.

What would George do if he saw Liz there with William? He'd probably keep his distance, given their history. But maybe not. Liz was confident that William would remain polite, perhaps retreating into cool silence. She didn't know George well enough to say how he'd react.

Jade and Carl headed toward a free table with William trailing behind. Liz veered off. If she greeted George now, she could mention she was there with other people, including William, so George could avoid their group.

By the time she got through the crowd to him, George had Lydia in his arms. The fluffy cat was rubbing her face on George's shoulder.

"Hi," Liz said. "Picking up the ladies already, I see."

He chuckled. "It's hard being popular."

"Yeah." Liz glanced over her shoulder. She couldn't see William through the crowd. "Anyway, I just wanted to say hi. I'm actually here with some people."

George's eyebrows went up. "Do you have room for one more?"

"Well, the thing is, I'm here with William, Carl, and my friend Jade. And I know you don't get along with William, so ..."

The eyebrows dipped down into a scowl. "I thought I warned you about him."

"Mm. It's a long story, but I was kind of forced into getting to know him. I like him, actually." A lot, but George didn't need to hear that.

"I guess you don't know him very well yet. Come on, hang out with me this evening. I promise I'll show you a much better time than he could."

People were finding seats. George looked toward the table with her friends and his lip curled.

"I don't judge your friend for setting her sights on Carl," he said. "She could do worse. But William is a stuck-up stuffed shirt. He's our age but acts about eighty. Look at him over there. He clearly doesn't want to be here. I'm amazed Carl was able to drag him here with all the cats."

Liz wasn't sure whether she wanted to defend William, verbally smack George for his comment about Jade, or just turn around and walk away. All the possible responses got tangled together and nothing came out.

George shifted so Liz had to turn in order to see him, putting her back toward her friends.

George lifted Lydia up to eye level. The cat drooped over his hands and mewed. "I ought to go shove you in William's face and see how he reacts."

"You're not supposed to pick up the cats!" Liz snapped.

"Oh, right." George brought Lydia back to his chest and chuckled. "Clearly Lydia doesn't mind me, but I guess other people might get a smack across the face. Some people say cats are unfriendly, but I say they're friendly with the right people." George's smile invited her in on the joke. "Right?"

"I don't know," Liz said. "I think it has more to do with the cats' temperament. Some are friendly and some are shy and, I imagine, a few are jerks. As for Lydia—" She nodded at the cat in George's arms. "Apparently she likes men. All men and any men, which shows she isn't picky. In fact, she was all over William the first time he came here."

George's face froze into a mask. Or maybe it was revealing what was under the mask. He looked mean. "He's gotten to you, hasn't he? He's fooled you into believing his side of the story."

Liz blinked. "I didn't even know there was a story with competing sides. I don't think William has said a single word about you to me. But you've certainly said a lot about him, and his vicious dog. I'm starting to wonder if he ever had a mean dog."

"You saw the scar!"

"I did. I only have your word for it that William's dog caused it. And even if that part is true, there could be more to the story. Perhaps I *should* get William's side of things."

Lydia squirmed and hissed. George glanced down at her and gentled his hold. When he looked up at Liz again, he had the charming smile back in place—but now she saw his expression as crafty, the kind of look one got from men who offered to buy you a drink at a bar in hopes of getting you drunk enough to exhibit poor judgment.

"I guess I shouldn't be surprised," he said. "Money buys a lot in this town, including a clean reputation. I thought you were different—that you would see past the family's fortune to the real man underneath. I guess I was wrong."

Liz narrowed her gaze. "I am trying to see the real man underneath. I just happen to like what I see—with William, that is. You, on the other hand … I think we're done here. Don't contact me again."

She sensed George's furious stare focused on her back as she dodged tables. She'd misjudged George as badly as she'd misjudged William, but in the other direction. At least with George, she could block his number and avoid him. She had more important things to do than bother with someone like that.

Liz rejoined her friends. William did look rather wooden. Jade shot Liz a concerned look, but then Carl said something to her and she turned toward him. William and Liz were silent for a minute. She wasn't sure what, if anything, she should say.

Finally he said, "I didn't know you knew George."

"Not well." Liz hesitated. Downplay the connection? Interrogate William about their past?

It had taken long enough to get William to talk freely to her. She didn't want him to clam up again. Besides, maybe he should know what George was saying. And Liz wanted to know the truth.

"I met him here, actually, the same day I met you. He said you two have known each other since childhood."

William grunted.

"He also said your dog bit him. He showed us the scar."

"He's still singing that song?" William shook his head, his expression fierce. "We were twelve. He was teasing my dog—tormenting her. Yes, she bit him, but he brought it on himself. And in case he's been implying I had a big, fierce dog, Lucy was a beagle. George put up such a fuss that his parents called animal control to our house, insisting Lucy be put down." He paused, his throat working.

"I remember that," Carl broke in. "It was scary."

William nodded. "When we explained the situation, that George was trespassing and harassing Lucy, and animal control saw the supposedly vicious beast, we got away with a warning."

Liz felt queasy just from hearing the story. "I see. Thank you for telling me."

William looked around. "I hope he's not planning to adopt one of these cats. I wouldn't trust him with an animal."

"We can warn the owner later," Liz said. "But I think George was just showing off. You know that fluffy marshmallow cat, Lydia? She likes most men. I think George was using her to show me ... He was trying to convince me he was a good guy, because a cat likes him."

Jade bit her lip for a moment. "It's possible he's changed. He was just a kid back then."

"I guess," William said skeptically. "I've avoided him since then, so I don't really know him now. But I haven't heard anything to convince me to change my opinion."

"I don't know what to say." Liz spread her hands. "He seemed nice enough when we first met, but I've seen some red flags since then. If there's any chance he'd mistreat an animal, we should make sure he doesn't get one."

"Yeah." William ran a hand through his hair.

"I'll talk to Kari later." Jade sighed. "We can't take any chances. He'll have to prove he'll be a good owner before he can adopt."

The lights dimmed and the noise level in the room dropped. Jade and Carl sat back.

William turned to Liz and lowered his voice. "I can't prove my version of the story. Maybe he even believes he's right."

Liz shifted closer and whispered, "He shouldn't get away with talking about you like that. Even if he's not quite lying, he's certainly twisting the truth so people will feel sorry for him and dislike you."

"Did it work?"

"Not with me." Although it had worked longer than it should have. "But who knows who else he's told these stories? It's slander."

His breath brushed past her ear and his voice rumbled, setting up an echo in her chest. "It doesn't matter," he said. "Let him tell his version of things. I don't care about him."

I don't care about him either. I care about you.

She didn't let the words out. She needed to sit with them a while. Dismissing George was easy enough, now that Liz knew what was hidden under the superficial charm. William was another matter. Certainly she'd misjudged him in the beginning. She'd gotten past that. He was a decent person—a good person, kind and generous and thoughtful. You just had to take the time to see it, because he didn't show off any of that.

The movie started playing. Liz and William sat in silence, but Liz's attention wasn't on the movie. It was on the man next to her.

Chapter 19

Liz tried to pay attention to the movie, but it wasn't easy. She found herself leaning closer to William, as if wanting to borrow some of his warmth. When she realized what she was doing, she shifted back, only to find herself doing it again. Meanwhile, her mind went in circles over her poor judgments of William and George. Where else has she failed? Could she have misjudged Dr. Collins as well? Had she made a mistake turning down that postdoc?

No. She was pretty sure she'd run screaming from his lab within two days.

The cats were also distracting. A few of them settled in laps, but others wrestled or chased toys or randomly decided to race around the room. At one point Lydia sashayed over and jumped into William's lap. He stiffened, and Liz reached for the cat.

"It's fine," he whispered. "Let's see what happens." He slowly relaxed and placed a hand on her head, one corner of his mouth pulling up in a smile.

That lasted a few minutes. Then Lydia put her paws on William's chest and pushed her head up under his chin. He made a choked coughing sound.

Liz pulled the cat off him. "Shoo. Go bother someone else."

Lydia meowed loudly and stalked off with her fluffy tail held high. A few heads turned at the sound. George was silhouetted against the movie screen, his sneer visible against the brighter background.

Liz tried again to focus on the movie. She didn't even notice the rain splattering the windows until William leaned over and whispered, "Guess we shouldn't have walked."

The movie ended and the lights went on. People got up to chat or play with cats. Some went back to the café counter for food or drink.

Jade sighed. "I guess I'll talk to Kari now."

William peered out the window. "I'll run home and get the car. No reason for all of us to get wet."

It was a strange echo of that day when George had given Liz and Jade a ride. He was standing alone, watching them. Liz glanced away. The café felt warm and stuffy. Maybe she should go with William, if only to get away from George and her own thoughts. But running through the rain in the dark sounded chilly and bleak rather than romantic.

Romantic? Where had she gotten that thought?

William grabbed his jacket and took off before Liz decided what to do. She moved to a corner where a sleek black and white cat sat on the padded bench. The cat watched curiously as Liz eased closer, holding her hand out and murmuring encouragement until she was close enough to stroke the smooth head. The cat pushed his head into her hand and purred.

Some of her tension drained away. Still, she'd rather be back at Carl's house with her friends. Or even better, at William's house, with Sausage and the dogs. William now kept his bedroom and office doors closed and let Sausage roam the rest of the house. The cat and the two dogs could often be found in a cuddle puddle together. What could be better than a cozy house, a kind man, a few pets, and maybe some hot cocoa as they all curled up on the couch?

George's voice jolted her out of her thoughts. "Does anyone know why William was carrying Lydia out of here?"

Liz swung around. George was addressing the room in general, apparently, from near the door. His hair and jacket glinted with moisture, so he must have gone outside and come back in.

"What are you talking about?" Carl said. "William didn't take a cat out of here."

George shrugged. "He was carrying one through the parking lot. I thought that was odd. For one thing, he doesn't like cats, and for another, I'm pretty sure the application process is longer than that." He radiated confidence and charm. It made the hair on the back of Liz's neck stand up.

Kari set her hands on her hips. "Lydia, you said?" She looked around the room. "She does like men. Maybe she followed him and slipped through the door."

"It may have started that way," George said, "but why was he carrying the cat away from here instead of bringing her back?"

Kari studied him skeptically. "Before we panic, let's make sure she's not actually still inside. Brian, you didn't put her in the office, did you?"

The boy shook his head. "She was in here a few minutes ago."

Kari and a few other people started searching. George met Liz's gaze from across the room. He spread his hands, miming helpful innocence. She didn't like his smirk.

For a cat to follow someone outside, it would have to get out of the café room unnoticed. Then it would need to either go through both doors at the foyer, or else slip through the back door as someone left. That part was possible, though unlikely given the number of people around and the warning signs on the doors asking people to look for sneaky cats. And Lydia didn't seem like the kind of cat that would willingly go out into the rain, even to follow a man—not when so many other men were still inside.

Even if Lydia had gotten out, the idea that William would carry a cat away from the café didn't make sense. George was a known liar. Therefore, George was lying.

When he left again, Liz followed. He headed for the back door. She waited half a minute and then slipped out after him.

She didn't see him in the parking lot. She did hear a meow, or more accurately an annoyed yowl. Where was it coming from? Maybe the part about Lydia escaping was true.

Or had George intentionally let the cat out?

Surely not. Whatever his flaws, he seemed to like Lydia well enough. He wouldn't simply let her loose on the streets, with all its dangers. Would he?

Liz crouched to look under the cars. It was too dark to see much, with only a couple of lights at the corners of the parking lot. She fumbled in her pocket for her phone so she could use the flashlight app.

An engine purred as a car backed out of its spot. The rear end swung around into Liz's view. She recognized George's sports car and stayed in a squat out of sight of the driver.

The yowling got louder as the car backed toward her. Then it faded as George pulled out of the parking lot.

For a moment Liz couldn't move. Then she pushed to her feet and stared after the car as it turned out of sight. No more cat yowling.

That cat had been in George's car. And it hadn't been happy about it.

She wanted to run after them. She wouldn't catch up on foot, so she hurried back inside.

Most of the customers had left. Kari and a couple of other staff members conversed in worried tones. Jade and Carl stood a few feet away, his arm around her. When Liz joined them, Jade said, "We can't find Lydia anywhere."

"William wouldn't have taken her," Carl added.

"No, but I think George did." Liz quickly explained.

Jade looked troubled. "But why? Did he realize we were warning Kari about him? Did he want to adopt Lydia so badly that he stole her?"

"And threw the blame on William." Carl frowned. "If George wanted a cat so badly, I'm sure he could've found one somehow. So maybe this is more about making William look bad."

Liz hugged herself and rubbed her arms, chilled from her brief trip outdoors. "Where would George take Lydia then? To his house? I hope he doesn't let her go outside."

Jade gasped. "Surely not!"

Liz managed a smile for her friend. "No, if he was going to do that, he could have let her go here." Unless he was taking Lydia farther away so no one looking around the café would find her. But upsetting Jade wouldn't help the situation.

"Either way, we need to find him, and Lydia," Carl said.

"I'll explain to Kari." Jade joined that group.

Liz and Carl listened to the discussion. All the employees had walked to the café to leave room for customers to park. They also had tasks to do before they could close up.

"William will be back with his car any minute," Carl said. "We'll find Lydia."

Kari nodded. "Jade has my number. Call us as soon as you know anything. If we can prove he took Lydia, that's a matter for the police. But the most important thing is to get her back safely."

Liz, Jade, and Carl headed outside to wait for William. The temperature had dropped since their pleasant walk over, and Liz envied Jade and Carl as they huddled together. She wouldn't mind sharing warmth with someone.

Not someone. A particular person. He'd been gone maybe fifteen minutes, and she missed him.

She tried to focus on the problem. "I guess we go to George's house first. But do we know where he lives?"

"I think I know his apartment building," Carl said. "At least where he was a couple of years ago." He pulled out his phone. "I'll see if I can confirm his current address."

When William pulled up, they piled in, Carl taking the front passenger seat.

William gestured to a pile in the middle of the back seat. "I grabbed a couple of jackets and blankets in case anyone's cold."

"I'm turning on map directions," Carl said. "We'll explain on the way."

"Okay." William looked at Carl's phone and pulled forward. "Explain what?"

Carl glanced back at Liz. She took a deep breath and went through the story again. She couldn't see much of William from the back of the dark car, but he radiated tension.

"This is my fault," William said. "If he didn't hate me so much ..."

"It's not!" Liz said.

Jade leaned forward to squeeze his shoulder. "He chooses to hate you. He must be terribly unhappy if he spends his time trying to hurt other people, but it's not your fault."

"But if I had done ..." William trailed off. "If I'd warned people about him earlier ... But I didn't know he was still carrying so much of a grudge."

"You can't even figure out what you should have done differently," Liz said. "Leave the blame where it belongs."

They pulled up to George's address. Liz and Jade grabbed coats from the pile as they got out.

"I don't see his car." Liz slid her arms into the sleeves of the oversized coat. It smelled of William. She breathed deeply and felt calmer.

Jade looked around. "Maybe he had to park down the street."

"Let's ring the bell," Carl said. "How do we get him to let us in? He won't want to, if he has Lydia with him."

"I'll do the talking." Liz wasn't sure what she would say. She didn't feel like playing games. She felt like marching up to George, giving him a piece of her mind, and snatching Lydia away. But first they had to get in and find Lydia. "I'll tell him ... I guess I'll pretend I believed his claims about William taking Lydia, and I need more information. If I get him to open the door, we push our way in and search the place."

"Is that legal?" Jade asked.

"At this point, I don't really care," Liz said. "If he wants to call the police, let him."

They hurried to the apartment building and clustered in the foyer. Liz found the button to buzz George's apartment and pushed it. They stared at the intercom, waiting. After half a minute that felt like an hour, Liz jabbed it again and held it down.

Still no response.

"Maybe he knows it's us," William said. "He could have been looking out the window."

Carl stretched a hand toward the panel of buttons. "Someone will let us in the building."

"Wait." Jade peered through the glass front door. "Someone's coming. I think it's him."

They went through a moment of panicked shuffling—there really wasn't any place to hide—before giving up and watching the door.

Jade pushed it open as George reached it.

He grinned. "Visitors? To what do I owe the pleasure?"

Forget pretense. It wouldn't work anyway, since George had seen William in the group. Liz stepped forward. "I heard Lydia in your car. Where is she?"

His eyes opened wide, the picture of surprise, but he was overdoing it. "I don't know what you mean. I told you, I saw William carrying her away." His mouth pulled into a sneer as he looked at William.

"We don't believe you," Liz said.

"If anything happens to Lydia ..." Jade scowled at George.

He chuckled. "Look at you, like a fierce little kitten."

Carl made a wordless sound of anger.

George held up his hands. "Okay, look, clearly I don't have Lydia with me." He pulled open his coat. "See, nothing in my pockets, nothing up my sleeves."

"How about in your car?" Liz asked.

George rolled his eyes. "Fine. Let's go."

They followed him out, but Liz's heart had already sunk. If he was that willing to let them search his car, Lydia probably wasn't there.

George unlocked the car with his key fob and stood back. Liz checked the trunk first. She found only a duffel of gym clothes, a small toolbox, and a roll of paper towels. She even peeled up the panel covering the spare tire well to discover ... the spare tire. She looked up and shook her head.

Jade and Carl opened the car doors and searched under the seats. William stood on the sidewalk a couple of feet away, looking stiff and uncomfortable.

George met Liz's eyes. "See? You should be careful about who you believe."

She stared back. "I know who to believe." And there was pale fur in his trunk, but she didn't mention that. They might be able to use it to prove George had taken Lydia, so she didn't want George to think of trying to clean the trunk.

George's smile dropped away and his jaw clenched.

Jade and Carl closed the car doors. "Nothing," Carl said.

"Like I told you." George turned toward his building, calling back over his shoulder, "I hope you find her. You might try looking at the real villain around here. Time will prove me right soon enough."

They watched him go into the building.

Carl gave a grunt of frustration. "Now what? If he let her go somewhere outside ..."

Liz's mind raced. What did George want? To make William look bad. Would he have stopped at stealing Lydia and letting her go? His last comment ...

"I have an idea," she said.

Chapter 20

"What?" Jade asked.

Liz waved them toward William's car. "Let's get in. I'll tell you on the way."

Could she be right? If not … But maybe she was!

She and Jade scrambled into the back seat while Carl took shotgun again.

"On the way where?" William asked.

"Home. Your place, I mean." Liz tried to organize her thoughts as the car pulled out. "Okay. It doesn't look like George wanted to keep Lydia. He just wanted to make William look bad."

"So he left her outside somewhere?" Jade wailed.

"Hang on," Liz said. "At the end there, George said something about how we'd soon see the real villain. To him, that means William. I think he took Lydia to William's house."

The others were silent. Liz held her breath, waiting for someone to poke holes in her argument. If she was wrong, then Lydia was probably outside somewhere, at best, and they wouldn't find her except through sheer good luck. Lydia's friendliness might help, or it might hurt if it drew her to dangerously busy areas.

"I was just at my house," William said. "Everything was normal."

"Just long enough to pick up your car, right?" Liz asked. "Did you even go inside?"

"Yeah, to grab the jackets, but that's all. The dogs greeted me." He thought for a moment. "I didn't notice George or his car, but I wasn't really looking."

Carl twisted around to look at Liz. "I hope you're right, but I'm not sure I understand the point. Why would George do that?"

"For one thing, it would support George's claim that William took the cat."

"We wouldn't believe him," Jade said.

"Thanks," William murmured.

"We wouldn't," Liz agreed. "But I bet George could convince himself otherwise. He thinks he's charming. He thinks William isn't." Her face heated, remembering how she'd thought that once.

Carl gave a thoughtful *hmm*. "You're right about that. And William has never tried to challenge George's claims."

"It seemed childish," William protested. "I don't want to get caught up in that kind of gossip."

Carl gave his friend a fond look. "I know. You took the high road, but that meant George had Main Street. I'm sure plenty of people were skeptical of his claims, but he's apparently been making those claims for almost twenty years. Even people who didn't believe him probably just ignored him instead of arguing. All that time going unchallenged? Liz is right. In his mind, you *are* the villain."

Liz leaned forward, nodding. "And now all of us know the truth, and we might tell other people. It's not just that his lies are being exposed. We saw through him, which attacked his view of himself. He must be desperate to 'prove' he's right, not only to us and whoever else, but to himself."

William paused at a stop sign and glanced back at her. "You got all this insight from studying worms?" His voice was laced with humor and ... could that be tenderness?

Jade was bouncing with nerves. "So he might think people would believe him about William, if he provides evidence. And dropping Lydia at William's house is the evidence?"

"That's my hope," Liz said.

Jade shook her head. "His plan doesn't make any sense. Why would William steal a cat instead of going through the adoption process? That's even assuming he wanted a cat. George surely doesn't know that William has started allergy treatments to build up his tolerance."

They had turned down William's street, and she hadn't

finished explaining. She couldn't prove this next part—probably never would be able to—but it felt right to her.

"George keeps saying William has a vicious dog," she said. "He may even believe it at this point, no matter that the dog that bit him is long gone. Remember, he wants to make William look bad. Taking a cat from the café is bad, but taking one so your mean dog can harass it ..."

Jade gasped.

William snorted out a laugh. "Sorry. It's not funny. But the thought of Rufus attacking a cat ... I'd put money on Lydia being the dominant one there. And Sadie wouldn't hurt a fly. Well, actually she likes to chase flies. But I don't think she'd hurt a cat. She gets along with Sausage well enough."

"I know," Liz said. "We got lucky. Or not *lucky*, since you chose and raised Rufus. George's plan will fail, because he doesn't know Rufus and Sadie, or you, or any of us."

She just hoped Lydia was still there when they arrived. No need to say that out loud. They were almost home. *William's* home. She needed to stop thinking of it as home, no matter how homey it felt.

William slowed as he turned into his driveway. "Keep an eye out in case she's outside."

Liz peered into the darkness. William's street had no streetlights, just a few pools of light from porches. For a moment Liz thought she saw eyes reflecting the car's headlights from the bushes beside his porch. Before she could say anything, they winked out. That could've been anything—a wild animal, her imagination. If she was right about George, he wouldn't have merely left Lydia in front of the house, where she could wander off. He'd want her found inside, preferably terrified if not actually injured.

William parked and they got out. The group was silent and solemn as they trooped up to the front door. William pulled out his keys.

"How would George have gotten inside?" Jade whispered.

"He wouldn't need to," Liz whispered back. "There's a dog door in the back. He could have gone around the house and shoved Lydia through it."

"Why are we whispering?" Carl whispered.

They started snickering, part amusement but mostly nerves.

William opened the door. The hall light was already on. Liz couldn't see past William, but she heard the quick tappity tap of dog fingernails on the floor. William stepped forward, making room for the rest of them to enter. He crouched to greet Sadie, the elderly poodle. The dog's tail whipped back and forth.

"Hi, girl." William rubbed her head with both hands. "Where's Rufus?" He stood up.

Sadie trotted toward the living room with a glance back over her shoulder. The humans followed her. They stepped inside to see the bulldog lying in his big bed with his head on his front paws. Rufus gave a low moan. It looked like he had a white and cream fur hat perched on his back. Then Lydia yawned and stretched. She blinked at the people, stood up with a meow, and delicately stepped off the dog and toward William. He looked down at her, shaking his head. Rufus sat up and wagged his stubby tail. Sadie licked Rufus's face.

"Oh, thank goodness!" Jade swooped in to pick up the cat. Lydia grumbled.

William slid his arm around Liz's shoulders. "You were right."

She was getting to know his smiles. They were subtle, more in the eyes than on the mouth, and all the more precious because she'd learned to see them when most people missed them. She read relief in his expression, and amusement, and admiration. Maybe even affection. For her?

"We'll take Lydia back to the café," Jade said. "No need for all of us to go."

Liz tore her gaze away from William to see Jade and Carl watching them. Carl was grinning. Jade looked smug.

William's arm tightened across Liz's shoulders and then slid away. She just had time to miss it before his hand settled against her lower back. Her body leaned into him without her mind's conscious thought.

"Thanks." He held out his keys. "Take my car. Come back here after? I think we all deserve a glass of wine, or maybe hot cocoa to warm us up. If I had champagne, I'd suggest a toast to Liz for being so clever."

Her face heated. "You would have found her here eventually."

Jade hugged the disgruntled-looking cat closer. "Yes, but you saved us the stress of searching the city because we wouldn't have thought to check here first."

"And you brought Sausage into my life." William nodded toward the sofa. The dark cat perched on the back of it like a loaf, watching them with sleepy eyes.

"I don't imagine Rufus and Sadie would have attacked a cat anyway," William added, "but they had a chance to get used to Sausage before Lydia showed up."

Carl winked at Liz. "There's no getting around it. You're a hero." He tossed the keys in his hand and glanced at Jade. "Let's get going. The sooner we drop her off, the sooner we're back for that drink. I'll drive and you can text Kari that we're on our way. She can decide whether she wants to call the police on George."

"It's going to be hard to prove anything," Jade said.

"Yes, but at least we can warn the animal rescue community," Carl said as they walked out.

"And Lydia's fur is in his trunk!" Liz called after them.

"Oh, that should help," Carl said.

The door shut behind them. Sadie stretched out alongside Rufus. Sausage's eyes were closed. William didn't move, so neither did Liz.

Finally he spoke. "You're pretty amazing, you know."

She turned toward him, keeping their bodies close. "You're not so bad yourself."

His hands settled on her hips. "The last couple of months have changed my life."

She tried to raise one eyebrow, although she suspected the other came along for the ride. "Extra dogs, cats in the house, and a judgmental woman thinking the worst of you until she learned better?"

"New friends, both humans and pets. A kick in the rear to start allergy treatments. And I'd say snarky rather than judgmental." He pulled her closer. "In case you're wondering, I like snarky women."

She lifted her face toward his. "Do you?"

"Mm. My absolute favorite." His lips brushed hers.

She swayed against him, holding on as the kiss deepened.

Yes. This was home.

Chapter 21

A month later, Liz stood at the front of a classroom to defend her PhD dissertation. Benjie and Dr. Bennett were there, with her third advisor listening via teleconferencing. The defense was open to the public, so she had a few people from her department attending, as well as her friends. As she went over the material, it was comforting to glance at Jade, William, or Carl and see their encouraging looks. They probably didn't follow half of what she said, but they believed in her, and that's what counted. Cheyenne and Nash were there too. That didn't exactly put Liz at ease, even though she'd been accepted as a volunteer at Big Cat Rescue, contingent on her staying in town.

After she finished her presentation, she took questions. Dr. Bennett used the opportunity to slide in a few digs, but Liz thought she handled everything with reasonable grace. It was a lot easier to be graceful when her freedom shone just outside the door.

Then Cheyenne raised her hand. At Liz's nod, she said, "Could your study techniques work on larger animals?"

"Interesting question," Liz said. "There are certainly different challenges. The larger the animal, the harder it is to keep a big group of them in captivity. You need the proper enclosures, people to care for them, money for vet bills, and much more. Plus, animals might behave differently in captivity than in the wild. But if you do the study in the wild, that has its own complications, as you know. Either way, with large animals, you'd probably get to know them as individuals, which means you can't really do a double-blind study."

She could have gone on for an hour, since she'd spent many hours thinking about the topic, but Dr. Bennett gave a pointed look at her watch.

Liz tried to wrap up without dropping the question too quickly. "Some zoos are studying elephant learning and cooperation. They set up a challenge where two elephants have to work together to pull a rope at the same speed in order to get a treat. So you can certainly study intelligence, or cooperation or whatever, in large animals. But it's not quite the same as working with worms."

She answered a few more questions. Finally the session wrapped up and people came to congratulate her. Liz was glad she'd applied deodorant with a heavy hand. She still felt shaky and a bit sweaty, but at least she didn't stink, as far as she could tell.

Benjie clasped her hand warmly. "Great job. I'm sure the committee will approve your dissertation." He winked and wandered off.

Dr. Bennett left without speaking to Liz, but she'd already grudgingly approved the written dissertation. A few other people from Liz's department congratulated her.

Finally she was alone with her friends. To her surprise, that group now seemed to include Cheyenne and Nash.

"What are your plans now?" Cheyenne asked.

"I don't know. I turned down one postdoc position, which might have been a mistake. No, actually, it definitely wasn't a mistake."

Dr. Collins sent her weekly emails with a dozen photos of Charlotte and long, rambling messages about his time with the cat. It was rather sweet, but she didn't need to see him in person every day.

"But there aren't a lot of other positions out there," Liz said, "and I don't want to move across the country."

Her work was important, but she was discovering how important it was to have friends, and a man like William, in her life. She didn't want to start over somewhere new.

"What's your dream job?" Cheyenne asked. "Do you want to become a college professor, either a teacher or a research professor? Or do research in the field?"

Liz hesitated. "I used to want to spend my life doing research in the field. You know, like Jane Goodall. But now ..."

She couldn't help looking at William, a warm, strong presence beside her. He was proud of her, not just for what she did but for who she was as a person. He wanted her to have what she wanted to have, what made her happy, and didn't care if she reached some supposed peak of a potential career.

"I don't want to spend my life somewhere else," Liz said. "Going into the field for a month or two would be fine, but I just finished almost a decade of school where I was always working. It would be nice to have a job with somewhat regular hours and time for other things. I don't want to spend my whole life at work anymore." She gave a wry smile. "That probably leaves out both fieldwork and becoming a college professor."

Cheyenne nodded. "I definitely get that. I loved my years in the field, but they are hard on the body and mind. And not great for relationships either." She leaned against Nash, her gaze still on Liz. "Even if you have a relationship with somebody doing the same fieldwork, it's hard to make sure you're always working in the same place at the same time. And of course you never get a break from work talk then."

"But your work talk is fascinating," Nash murmured.

"Well, of course." Cheyenne flashed him a flirtatious look. "I still appreciate the occasional reminder that there is more going on in the world."

Liz nodded. "There's a lot to consider. I need to find some kind of job though."

"You know you have a place to stay as long as you need," Carl said.

William's hand touched her lower back and rubbed a little circle. Liz took that as his agreement.

Jade hooked her arm through Carl's, looking at Liz with an expression that said, Isn't he great?

Perhaps it was easy for Carl to be generous, given how often Liz stayed at William's house now, but she gave him a grateful smile. She was still getting used to people who wanted her to be happy and were willing to help without expecting anything in return. She hoped she didn't get so used to it that she took it for granted. Privately, she thought Caroline was so spoiled because she came from a moderately wealthy family and had Carl to step in whenever she made a mistake. But at least the girl was focusing more on school and her social life there, now that she'd given up on snagging William.

"I've been missing field research," Cheyenne said. "But at the same time, not, for the reasons you mentioned. I wonder if we could conduct research at the rescue while maintaining the focus on caring for the animals and giving them as much of a natural life as possible."

Liz buzzed as if hit by an electric shock. "That would be exciting. I'm sure there are ways ..." She trailed off, her mind already racing.

"Write up a proposal," Cheyenne said. "No rush—take time to celebrate your success today. But when you're ready, and if you're interested in leading a research project ..."

Liz nodded rapidly, too overcome to speak.

"Put something together and let me know. I'll talk to the money guys." She nudged Nash, who grinned, apparently not upset by the suggestion. "Congratulations." Cheyenne and Nash headed out, leaving Liz with just William, Jade, and Carl.

Liz took a moment to simply breathe, slowly filling her lungs with air and letting it out, along with the stress of the day—and at least a little of the stress of the last decade.

"How do you feel?" Jade asked.

Liz shook her head. She didn't know how to answer.

"It's okay if you feel lost," Carl said. "When you've been working on something for such a long time and it ends, it can take a while to get used to the new reality."

William simply tightened his arm around her and pressed a kiss to her temple.

"Yeah," Liz said. "It might take a while before I

completely believe it's over. But it is, and it sounds like I have the possibility of work here, which is ..." She took a deep breath. "I don't even know how to explain it. It's like I've been churning away in some kind of purgatory for years, and I finally escaped!"

They chuckled.

Liz blinked back tears. "I feel so lucky."

"It's not luck." William held her close against his side. "You did this."

"It's a little luck," Liz said. "Maybe a lot of luck, along with a lot of hard work, and maybe that's the only way you get anywhere. I'm not complaining. I'll take the luck."

"Me too." Jade grinned. "Who would've thought the destruction of our bathroom ceiling was lucky?"

"Hey," Liz said, "I'd prefer to avoid building collapses in the future, no matter how lucky. But yeah, it turned out all right."

What if she'd never gotten to know William, because she trusted her first impression? What if he hadn't been willing to give her another chance? What if George had succeeded in fooling them all?

Too many *what ifs*. What mattered now was the reality.

"Let's get out of here," she said. "I'm ready to celebrate. Everything else can wait."

After all, she had the rest of her life.

Chapter 22

Liz hung up the phone. She took a couple of deep breaths, until she was able to let go of some annoyance. Who cared what anyone else thought about the way she lived her life? She had work she loved, good friends, pets to cuddle, and William.

She found him in the living room. He tossed the newspaper on the coffee table and patted the sofa next to him. The dogs lay curled together in the big dog bed on the floor. Sausage was snoozing on the back of the sofa, his favorite place now that he had lost enough weight to get up there easily.

Liz sat next to William, tucking her legs up so she was turned to face him. "Anything interesting in the paper?"

"Yeah, in the local. George plea bargained for community service."

"Right, Jade told me. It's good, I guess. I don't think jail time would change him. At least this way he takes responsibility for what he did, and people know what he's really like. Did it say where he's going to do his community service?"

"No." William tucked a strand of Liz's hair behind her ear. "You look smug. What do you know?"

"Jade told me he's going to work at the cat rescue. Not hers, but the main one."

"That's a little weird."

"Yeah, but Jade and the other rescue workers hope he'll learn something. About the work they do and the dangers feral cats face on the streets, I guess. I don't know, maybe he'll learn some empathy. If nothing else, the shelter gets free labor. I do like the idea of George having to clean cages and change litter boxes."

She rubbed Sausage's ears. The cat yawned, stretched, and slithered down between Liz and William to sprawl across their laps. William's allergy treatment had worked well enough that he wasn't bothered by one cat anymore, so they had adopted Sausage permanently. William could even visit Carl and Jade, who had turned two rooms of their house into the special needs cat rescue.

It was hard to believe everything that had happened in only a few months. The management company for their old apartment had finally made a decent settlement with the residents, but Liz and Jade had never bothered to find a new place to live. Or rather, Liz had gradually moved her things over to William's, until she was living there full-time. It was so easy and fun to have the four of them close together, spending evenings drinking wine on the back porch or barbecuing while the dogs played. Occasionally they all helped with bottle-feeding a batch of kittens. Using part of Carl's house for her rescue meant Jade was entirely intertwined with Carl, but even cynical Liz couldn't argue with Jade's choice. The two were so obviously meant to be together. And with Caroline living on campus again and Liz at William's, they had enough room.

"How are your parents?" William asked.

Liz knew he'd get around to asking about her phone call eventually. "Still disappointed in me." She shrugged. "They'll get over it."

He scowled. "They have no right to be disappointed. You made your choices for good reasons. They should be proud!"

She snuggled up next to him. "Thanks. I'm happy where I am. We're already discovering things about big cat personality and behavior that will help zoos and other facilities improve conditions. I get to work with animals and do research, and I get paid for it! Not that much, granted, but probably as much as I'd make as an adjunct professor during the years I chased a tenure position. And I don't have to teach – or risk turning into another Dr. Bennett."

William made a horrified face. "That would never happen."

Liz could still envision that path, the one she'd almost taken. The one she would have taken, no matter how much she dreaded it, if she'd gone where other people pushed. She was still trying to forgive herself for taking so long to accept she was on the wrong path, but she had no doubt she'd made the right choice. For one thing, she wasn't angry and frustrated all the time. She woke up *looking forward* to each day.

William was part of that, of course. But so was her work and her free time.

"You won't hear any regrets from me," Liz said. "But my parents still think I should go back to academia. They also pointed out that if I got what they consider a real job, an academic job, I could pay for my own place. They think I shouldn't be living off a man."

He narrowed his gaze and punched one fist into the other hand in mock threat. "What man?"

She nudged him with her shoulder. "You know which one."

"You're not living off of me. That's nonsense."

"Well, you're not charging me rent."

"I was paying the mortgage for five years before you moved in. If I charged you rent, I'd be making money off of you."

"I know," Liz said. "Just tell me if you ever want to change the way we do things. I won't mind."

"Wait, is this one of those conversations I have to have out loud?"

Liz chuckled. "Ideally. Although I am getting better at reading you."

"Then I hope you know I'm proud of you, and I wouldn't change a thing about you or our relationship." His hand closed over hers, playing with her fingers. "At least ..."

She sat up straighter. "At least what?"

His cheeks went rosy. "Well, I wouldn't say no to marriage eventually."

Liz grinned. "Is that a proposal?"

"Maybe? No, if you want a proposal, I can do better than that. But I know we haven't been together that long."

She took his hand in both of hers. "Tell you what, when I'm ready to be engaged, *I'll* propose to *you*."

His face lit up. "Okay. Do you think you will be ready, one day?"

"Pretty sure." She leaned in to kiss him. "You know I love you, right?"

He rubbed his cheek against hers. "Yes, and I love you. You've made my life so much better. I'm so lucky to have you."

"Well, you're proud of me and want me to be happy the way I want to be. Jade's the only person I could say that about before."

"Guess you should've married her."

"Nah, she's too cheerful in the mornings. She sings." Liz shuddered. Then she leaned against him and rested her head on his shoulder. They each rested a hand on Sausage's back, their fingers loosely linked. "Anyway, this way our family is twice as big."

"And growing at an exponential rate, if you count the animals."

"I always count the animals."

The last tension from her parents' disapproval eased out of Liz. She had her PhD, which might help with getting grants for Big Cat Rescue, and could provide opportunities in the future if she ever decided to do something different. She had a family here that loved and supported her, people who found joy in animals and worked hard but not to the exclusion of everything else. She had William, and together they'd build a great future.

Dear Readers,

I hope you've enjoyed getting to know the gang at Furrever Friends. If so, **please leave a review!** Even a few lines help other readers find books they might enjoy. Reviews help authors find an audience, and they help readers find great books.

Special thanks to Pnina and Lucia for reviewing the manuscript for me.

The Furrever Friends Sweet Romance series features the employees and customers at a cat café. Watch as they fall in love with each other and shelter cats. Read the whole series:

Coffee and Crushes at the Cat Café – book 1
Kari doesn't have time for love when she's opening her new cat café. So what can she do when a sexy master baker walks in?

Kittens and Kisses at the Cat Café – book 2
He's loved her forever. She still sees him as the neighbor kid. Can five desperate kittens bring them together?

Tea and Temptation at the Cat Café – book 3
Can two lonely people carrying scars from the past get a second chance at finding love?

Romance and Rescues at the Cat Café – book 4
Can getting stranded in a creepy house full of abandoned cats turn these enemies into friends—or even something more?

Christmas Cookies at the Cat Café – book 5
Christmas isn't the same since Diane's kids grew up and her husband died – so when her high school sweetheart comes back to town, maybe it's time for some cozy new holiday traditions.

Cupcakes and Confessions at The Cat Café –6
Fiona gave up her baby for adoption 23 years ago. When Sean notes how much she looks like his coworker, Fiona is suddenly reunited with her grown-up daughter. Sean steadies Fiona through this emotional roller coaster, but she doesn't have room for romance – does she?

Next up, the recipes for **Quick Pasta Arrabbiata, Key Lime Poundcake with Key Lime Cream Cheese Frosting** and **Cranberry Pistachio Biscotti** mentioned in this story. Then read on for a sample of *The Billionaire Cowboy's Christmas*: The Accidental Billionaire Cowboys 1, plus a sample of my humorous mystery, *Something Shady at Sunshine Haven*.

—Kris Bock

Key Lime Poundcake with Key Lime Cream Cheese Frosting

This delicious, rich poundcake is even better a day or two later, so you can make it ahead for parties or dinner guests!

4 sticks of butter (1 pound), at room temperature
3 cups sugar
6 large eggs, room temperature
1/2 cups fresh key lime juice
1/4 cup evaporated milk
4 tsp key lime zest
1 tsp vanilla
4 cups all-purpose flour
See Icing ingredients on the next page

1. Preheat oven to 300°. Spray the inside of 10-inch tube pan with non-stick spray.
2. Using a mixer, beat the butter until it is fluffy. Add the sugar and beat again for at least 5 minutes.
3. Add the eggs one at a time, beating for a few seconds after each one.
4. In a small bowl, mix the key lime juice, evaporated milk, lime zest, and vanilla.
5. Add the flour a cup at a time to the butter-egg mixture, alternating with the key lime mixture. Mix by hand just enough to incorporate all ingredients.
6. Pour the batter into the pan. Tap the pan on the counter to release any air bubbles.
7. Bake for 1 hour and 45 minutes, until a cake tester or toothpick comes out clean.
8. Cool in the pan on a cooling rack for about 20 minutes. Then turn out the cake on the cooling rack and cool for one hour. Frost the cake when it's completely cool.

Key Lime Cream Cheese Icing

8 ounces cream cheese at room temperature
3-4 tablespoons butter at room temperature
4 cups confectioner's sugar
1/4 cup key lime juice
1 tablespoon key lime zest
1 teaspoon vanilla extract

1. Beat the cream cheese and butter in a large bowl until blended.
2. Add the confectioner's sugar. Beat until smooth and fluffy.
3. Add the other ingredients and mix well.
4. Frost the cake. You can fill the middle hole in the cake with any extra icing and add a spoonful to each slice when serving.

Cranberry Pistachio Biscotti

Biscotti get their firm, crispy texture from being baked twice. In fact, in Italian *biscotti* means "twice baked." Biscotti are often dipped in coffee to soften them.

1 3/4 cups flour, plus more if needed
2 teaspoons baking powder
1/4 teaspoon salt
1 teaspoon orange zest
1 cup sugar
1/4 cup cornstarch
3/4 cup orange juice
2 tablespoons butter, or use coconut oil for a vegan version
1 teaspoons almond extract or vanilla
1 cup dried cranberries
1 cup whole, shelled pistachios
2 tablespoons sugar to sprinkle on top

1. Preheat oven to 350°F.
2. In a medium bowl, stir together the flour, baking powder, salt, and orange zest. Set this mixture aside.
3. In a large bowl, stir together the sugar and cornstarch. Add the orange juice and blend with an electric mixer for about 3 minutes. Add the butter or coconut oil and the extract. Beat for another 3 minutes.
4. Blend the two mixtures. Stir in the cranberries and pistachios.
5. Form the dough into a ball. If the dough is too sticky, add flour a tablespoon at a time, up to 4 tablespoons, until you can form a firm ball.
6. Divide the dough into equal halves. Mold each ball into a log about 12 inches long by 3 inches wide by one inch high. Place each log on a baking sheet.
7. Sprinkle 1 tablespoon of sugar on top of each log.
8. Bake for 30 minutes. Cool on a wire rack for 15 minutes.

9. Use a cutting board and a serrated knife to cut the logs into 1-inch slices. Spread these slices on the baking sheets. Bake for 20 minutes at 350°F.
10. Cool the biscotti on a wire rack and store it in an airtight container.

Quick Pasta Arrabbiata (Angry Tomato Sauce)

Fiery spices make this zesty Italian sauce a favorite.
Serves 2

2 tablespoons olive oil
1 teaspoon crushed garlic
1 teaspoon red chili pepper flakes or more to taste
1 (14 1/2 ounce) can Italian-style pureed tomatoes
1 1/2 teaspoons minced garlic
salt to taste
1/2 pound pasta, such as penne
1/4 cup fresh parsley, chopped
1/4 cup fresh basil, chopped
Parmesan

1. Warm the olive oil in a deep frying pan on medium heat. Add the chili pepper flakes.
2. When the oil gets a little color from the chili, add the tomatoes, garlic, and salt. Cook 10-15 minutes, until the sauce thickens.
3. Meanwhile, cook the pasta according to package directions.
4. Combine the pasta, sauce, parsley, and basil. Top with parmesan.

Preview: The Billionaire Cowboy's Christmas: The Accidental Billionaire Cowboys 1 by Kris Bock

In the Accidental Billionaire Cowboys series, a Texas ranching family wins a billion-dollar lottery. They're advised to go into hiding, but they have animals needing care. They'll have to stay and fend off envious friends, scammers, and fortune hunters. Can they build new dreams and find love amidst the chaos?

Josh Tomlinson paused on the porch to shake water from his jacket and stomp the mud off his boots. He couldn't complain about rain in Texas. The grass needed it, and they needed grass to feed the livestock. But rain reminded him that the barn roof needed repairs. They also had to tear up the old cement slab that was rotting, level the ground, and pour a new slab. Even if he and his brothers did the labor themselves, they were looking at ten thousand dollars in materials. So yeah, rain wasn't his favorite thing right now.

Plus, some folks claimed a wet November meant a snowy December. What if they had another winter with those heavy snows and weeks of below freezing temperatures? Sure, snow was pretty, when you didn't have to work in it, with frozen hands and wind cutting through your jacket and trying to steal your hat, and when you didn't have to worry about how you were going to pay the heating bill and keep your family and all your animals alive and healthy.

Okay, maybe he could complain about the rain.

He stepped inside, hung up his jacket, and left his boots under the bench inside the front door. His mama sat at the big table in the main room straight ahead. To his right, the sofa faced the TV and formed the divider between the dining room and living room. His brother TC lounged on one end with his feet up, so he could see their mama at the table behind the sofa. Their youngest brother, Xander, sat on the other end with his laptop on his knees.

"Josh!" Mama looked up with a smile. "Come get warm."

He bent to kiss her cheek. They had their money troubles, being rich in land but poor in cash, like a lot of ranchers. But they were still here, at least most of them. Some of the tension left his shoulders as heat warmed his chilled skin.

"We're planning what we'll do when we win the lottery," TC said.

Josh merely grunted and went into the kitchen. Something simmered in the crockpot, giving off savory smells, but Josh headed for the coffeepot. It would be decaf this time of day, but it would warm him up. He filled his mug and went back to the table, sitting catty-corner from his mother.

"Come on, Xander," TC said. "You can come up with something better than that."

Xander didn't look up from his computer screen. "All I really need is a new computer."

"But we're talking a billion dollars!" TC said. "You could buy, like, a million computers."

"A billion is one thousand million. I could build a good computer for one thousand dollars, but it's more like thirty-five hundred for an excellent business computer. Call it four thousand dollars with software. So, I could buy a quarter of a million computers. But I only need one." Xander frowned for a few seconds. "Although it would be handy to have a full backup system in case something breaks."

Josh chuckled. Xander had earned the nickname the Professor when he graduated high school at fifteen. He'd been helping with the ranch's accounting since age twelve, annoying their father by finding math errors, until finally Daddy had handed over the financial records to Xander entirely. Thank goodness for that. Daddy had died when Josh, the oldest son, was only twenty-four. Josh had his hands full supporting Mama and trying to keep the ranch running. At least he could trust Xander with the numbers. TC did his share of the work but always had some crazy idea about how to make the ranch pay better. And Cody had taken off the minute he could, even before Daddy died.

"Why are we talking about billions of dollars anyway?" Josh asked.

Xander twisted around to look at him. "Only one billion."

"Oh, is that all?"

"What would you do with that kind of money, Josh?" TC asked.

"I don't know." Josh didn't see the point of thinking about impossibilities. "I suppose you'd buy your ostriches, or was it emus?"

"I would absolutely buy a herd of ostriches. Maybe emus as well. Also llamas, for the wool."

"Why are we talking about money we don't have?" Josh asked.

"Lottery," TC and Xander said together.

Josh turned to his mother. "Right, your knitting group met today. But if you'd won the lottery, I'd have heard about it already."

Mama held up one more ticket. "The group didn't win, but I bought an extra ticket for the family, since the amount is so high."

"You know that doesn't improve your odds," Xander said. "Anyway, the winner—assuming there is one this week—won't get that much all at once. The billion could be split among multiple winners, and then you have taxes."

A billion dollars? Josh's mind boggled. He could barely conceive of a tenth of that, a hundredth of that. Ten thousand dollars would take care of the ranch's immediate needs. One hundred thousand would let them make important improvements and keep some money in the bank for the future. People used phrases like a billion dollars when talking about the federal government's budget, not the finances of ordinary folks.

What about a million? He could almost grasp the idea of having that in the bank, since he knew a few people who were millionaires even without counting the value of their ranches. A million dollars must feel warm and comforting, like a thick blanket covering you up at the end of a long day when you'd finally, finally ticked everything off the to-do list. With that much, he could take care of the ranch, take care of Mama, give Xander his computers, and let TC play around with his giant birds.

But why would anyone need more than a million dollars, let alone a thousand million dollars?

"You know you're dreaming about things that will never happen." Josh reached over to squeeze his mother's hand to take the sting out of the words.

She laughed. "Oh, sweetie, I don't expect to win. But for a few minutes, we all get to dream."

"What would you buy with the money then?" Josh asked her. "If you became a billionaire."

She laughed again. "You mean if we became billionaires. You'd each get your share."

"Gosh, thanks." He had to smile at the idea of sharing their imaginary money. "But what about you? What would you want?"

She so rarely asked for anything. She hadn't even hinted at what she might like for Christmas. If she gave them some idea, and if they could make it happen . . . Something small enough . . .

"Oh, I don't know." She spread her hands. "Travel? See the world? I've never been outside of Texas."

Nothing he could buy her. Well, maybe a trip across the border, down to Mexico? Xander could go with her. TC and Josh couldn't leave the ranch unless they hired people to do the work in their absence, and they certainly couldn't afford that.

"Maybe I'd buy my own house, leave you boys the ranch," she mused. "Not too far away though, so I could see you every day, you and someday your wives and children."

"Sorry, Mama, I don't think you can buy us wives and children," TC said.

"Being rich wouldn't hurt your chances any," Mama said. "I can't believe I have two boys over thirty, and two in their twenties, and none of you even have a girlfriend—at least that you've told me!"

"Hey, I'm barely thirty," TC said. "Nag Josh. He's the old man."

Yeah, right, like he could afford a wife and kids.

"I don't know why you play the lottery if you want things money can't buy." Josh smiled at his mother, but his heart hurt. As the only woman living with three grown men—four when Cody visited—no wonder she wished for a daughter-in-law or two. She wasn't old, far from it, with plenty of brown amongst the gray in her hair, but with Daddy gone so early, she might wonder if she'd live long enough to see grandchildren.

But who had time for dating? His brothers, maybe, but not Josh. Anyway, he had enough people depending on him. He didn't need someone else to worry about, when he had three brothers and his mother to support.

Quick Peek: Something Shady at Sunshine Haven by Kris Bock

In The Accidental Detective humorous mystery series, a witty journalist solves mysteries in Arizona and tackles the challenges of turning fifty.

"Welcome home," Dad whispered.

"It's good to be home." I needed to rest and heal, and where better to do that than in my parents' house? In a few weeks—I promised myself weeks, not months, and definitely not years—I would be well enough to return to journalism. "How's Mom?"

"Good. Well, you know. She's settled in. She can't wait to see you."

I didn't ask if she'd remember me. I hadn't noticed signs of Alzheimer's on my last visit, but that had been a year ago.

"Hey, a friend of yours runs the care home," Dad said. "She gave me a message for you. Said it was urgent." He shuffled through the mail on the little table by the door and handed me an envelope. I leaned on the door and propped my cane against the table so I had two hands to tear open the envelope. The handwritten message inside was brief:

Kitty—Please come see me ASAP. I need your help.
—Heather Garcia

"She sounded . . ." Dad hesitated. "She asked about your journalism and begged me to bring you in as soon as possible. "We can go see your mother whenever you're ready," Dad said.

See Mom in a nursing home, literally losing her mind? I'd never be ready for that.

"No time like the present." Plus I could find out more about Heather Garcia's desperate plea for help.

After visiting Mom, I found Heather in her office.

"I have a problem," she said.

I tensed. "About Mom?"

"Oh, no, she's delightful, very popular with the staff and the other patients." Heather shuffled some papers on her desk. "No, this is . . . something else." She glanced at the closed door, leaned forward, and lowered her voice. "Can I tell you something in confidence?"

My journalism senses, dormant and neglected for weeks, gave a faint tingle before subsiding in exhaustion.

"It depends. I won't spread gossip. I hardly know anyone around here to tell." I smiled. "But if you confess to murdering someone, I'll have to report you."

"Ha. Nothing like that. I hope."

I stared at her. "You'd better tell me what's bothering you. If I can keep it a secret in good conscience, I will."

Her hands clenched on her desk. "I need to know that you're not here as a reporter."

I nodded and settled back into the chair with the trustworthy expression I'd mastered. Or possibly I simply looked tired. "This is off the record. I'm on leave anyway."

"Okay." She spread her fingers and pressed her hands on the desk. "Two of my patients died last week."

My stomach churned. People came to this place for the ends of their lives. My mother . . .

Shut down that thought. Snap into journalist mode.

It was more of an ooze than a snap, but I found a logical question. "Is that unusual?"

"Most of my patients are going to die here eventually, except those in the short-term care wing. Still, people can live for years with Alzheimer's and dementia, if they are otherwise healthy." Now she had the soothing, professional voice she'd no doubt perfected on hundreds of patients' families. "Our usual turnover is one every month or two."

"Two in a week could be a normal variation then." Good. I sounded calm, even if part of my mind still ran in circles screaming, "No! Not my mommy!" I cleared my throat and asked, "Was something suspicious about these deaths?"

She sighed. "Not exactly. I mean, they were old, but both women were in reasonable health and died suddenly. One complained of stomach pains and vomited a few times. The other seemed unusually weak and confused, according to the nurse who gave her medicine that evening. With Alzheimer's patients, it can be hard to identify a separate illness from the normal disease progression." Her voice wavered. "They were both dead by morning."

"The vomiting could be food poisoning. That can kill a person in poor health."

"These two incidents were a week apart, and no one else got sick either time. With food poisoning, you'd expect a wider outbreak."

I frowned. "What was the cause of death?"

"Officially, heart failure. We file death certificates, but unless the death is clearly questionable, no one would order an autopsy." She clenched her hands together. "One more thing. Two weeks ago, another woman got very ill, yet she recovered. Now she's fine. No one else in the unit got sick at the same time and we don't know what she had."

"Food poisoning seems unlikely with three patients sick that far apart," I admitted.

"One of these cases alone wouldn't worry me, but the three of them together . . ."

Alarm bells clamored in my mind. Was I reacting as a reporter or as a daughter? I dragged in slow, deep breaths to force back the nausea and become the logical, skeptical correspondent. I'd covered stories where hundreds or even thousands of people had died in natural disasters or acts of war. Two old women dying in a nursing home wasn't much of a story.

Except that my mother was now an old woman living in a nursing home. "What exactly do you suspect?"

"I'm probably being paranoid. But once in a while, you hear stories about a nurse or aide who decides the people in their care would be better off if they didn't have to suffer any more." She looked away and whispered, "How could I forgive myself if more people died because I wasn't willing to ask questions?"

"Have you talked to the police?"

"Definitely not." Her eyes pleaded with me. "It would be disastrous for the home. People would want to remove their parents and spouses. Even if these deaths were perfectly natural, the rumors would destroy us. I can't do nothing, but I also can't put the entire operation at risk over a vague possibility."

I couldn't argue with that. The press would love a story about a murdering caregiver, and a false rumor could taint a business for years. I suspected I knew the answer, but I asked, "What exactly do you want from me?"

"I'd like you to investigate. You're a journalist, you know how to find out things, and I trust you more than some random private detective. I want you to learn what happened, which hopefully will put my mind to rest. Am I being paranoid, or is someone killing my patients?"

About the Author

Kris Bock is the author of The Accidental Detective humorous mystery series, the Accidental Billionaire Cowboys sweet romance series, the Felony Melanie: Sweet Home Alabama romantic comedy novels.

In the Accidental Billionaire Cowboys series, a Texas ranching family wins a billion-dollar lottery. They're advised to go into hiding, but they have animals needing care. They'll have to stay and fend off envious friends, scammers, and fortune hunters. Can they build new dreams and find love amidst the chaos?

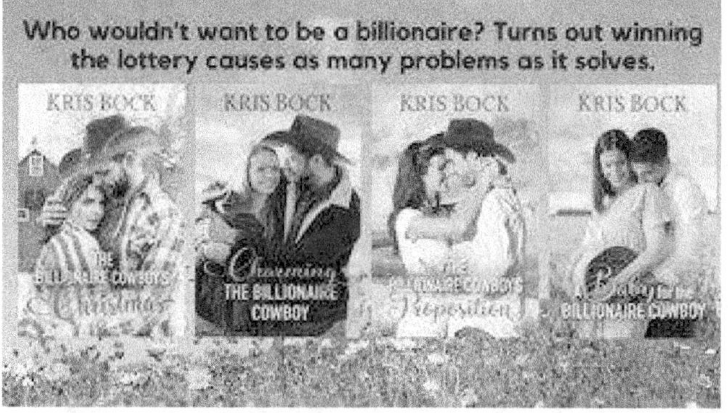

In The Accidental Detective humorous mystery series, a witty journalist solves mysteries in Arizona and tackles the challenges of turning fifty. Book 1 is Something Shady at Sunshine Haven: When patients are dying at an Alzheimer's unit, a former war correspondent must use her journalism skills to uncover the killer and save her mother. Kate has followed the most dangerous news stories around the world, but can she survive going home?

Kris also writes a series with her brother, scriptwriter Douglas J Eboch, who wrote the original screenplay for the movie *Sweet Home Alabama*. Follow the crazy antics of Melanie, Jake, and their friends a decade before the events of the movie.

Big City, Big Glamour, Big Trouble
Check out the new series featuring "Felony Melanie" a decade before the events of the movie *Sweet Home Alabama.*

Sign up for the Rom-Com newsletter at sendfox.com/lp/1rpny3 and get "Felony Melanie Destroys the Moonshiner's Cabin." These first two chapters from the novel *Felony Melanie in Pageant Pandemonium* stand alone as a short story. In the future, you'll get fun content about upcoming Felony Melanie novels and other romantic comedy news and links. Or find the series at all major book retailers.

Finally, Kris writes novels of suspense and romance with outdoor adventures and Southwestern landscapes.

Desert Gold follows the hunt for a long-lost treasure in the New Mexico desert. In *Valley of Gems*, estranged relatives compete to reach a buried treasure by following a series of complex clues. In *Silver Canyon*, sparks fly when reader favorites Camie and Tiger help a mysterious man track down his missing uncle. *Whispers in the Dark* features archaeology and intrigue among ancient Southwest ruins. *What We Found* is a mystery with strong romantic elements about a young woman who finds a murder victim in the woods. In *Counterfeits*, stolen Rembrandt paintings bring danger to a small New Mexico town.

Learn more at Kris Bock's website.

Pig River Press
Socorro, New Mexico
Copyright © 2024 Christine Eboch

www.ingramcontent.com/pod-product-compliance
Lightning Source LLC
Chambersburg PA
CBHW060918140726
47996CB00001B/302